SAYONARA, GANGSTERS

Genichiro Takahashi

translated by
Michael Emmerich

VERTICAL.

Published by Vertical, Inc., New York.

Originally published in Japanese as *Sayounara Gyangu-tachi* by
Kodansha, Tokyo, 1982.

ISBN 1-932234-05-5

Manufactured in the United States of America

First American Edition

Vertical, Inc.
257 Park Avenue South, 8th Floor
New York, NY 10010
www.vertical-inc.com

CONTENTS

Part One
In Search of "The Nakajima Miyuki Song Book"

Part Two
The Poetry School

Part Three
Sayonara, Gangsters

This translation is dedicated to the memory of Theodore Weiss

SAYONARA, GANGSTERS

"One After Another, Like Bowling Pins, U.S. Presidents Are Toppled by GANGSTERS"

—The New York Times

"Ladies and Gentlemen!

Even as I speak, evil GANGSTERS are scattering death and terror everywhere.

In London, in Paris, in Tokyo, in Leningrad, and in Cape Cook, Maryland, THE GANGSTERS continue to smash, pillage, and rape.

Ladies and Gentlemen!

THE GANGSTERS are cruel, brutish, and completely lacking in reason and humanity, and nothing pleases them more than to stamp their seal of death across the globe.

Ladies and Gentlemen!

I am grateful for the privilege of making this announcement, here and now.

I, John Smith Jr., President of the United States, make the following declaration to all the peace-loving citizens of America, and to the entire world.

We will wipe THE GANGSTERS clean off the face of the earth, swiftly and thoroughly, rooting them out, leaving no survivors.

The enemies of peace never win.

We will not falter in carrying out our noble mission.

In the name of the law, justice, and God.

Amen.
(Wild applause.)"

John Smith Jr. was the seventh U.S. president this year, and of the seven his time in office was the second shortest.

The 66th U.S. president, William Smith, died during his inauguration when, having placed his hand upon the Bible to take the presidential oath, he was bitten by a poisonous snake concealed inside. This was orchestrated by the gangsters.

The 69th U.S. president, John Smith Jr., died shortly after giving the historic speech in which he pledged to eradicate the gangsters; he was still surrounded by a circle of 100 Secret Servicepersons when the explosion occurred.

Henry Smith III, one of the Secret Servicepersons who witnessed the assassination at close range, described his last moments:

"The president had his right hand shoved down into his coat pocket when he came down the steps of the platform. He kept wiggling it around.

'Is anything wrong, Mr. President?'

'Yeah, I can't seem to find my . . .'

I knew immediately what it was the president was looking for.

The president was a great fan of Nabisco Bubble Gum. When he wasn't giving a speech or appearing on TV, he was always chomping it and blowing bubbles.

'Awesome! I had some after all!!'

The president extracted two Nabisco Bubble Gums from his back pocket.

'How 'bout it, Henry?' he said. 'It'll help you relax.'

'No, sir. Secret Servicepersons aren't permitted to chew

bubble gum on duty."

The president tore the wrapper off one piece of bubble gum and popped it into his mouth, then began unwrapping the second.

And then it happened.

I thought the president had sneezed. Yep, that's how it sounded.

An instant after the president bit down on that bubble gum, there was nothing on his shoulders but empty space.

I screamed 'Mr. President!' and threw my arms desperately around our president's headless body. He was still struggling to tear the wrapper off bubble gum number two."

Part One
In Search of "The Nakajima Miyuki Song Book"

I "Thank you"

1.

Once upon a time, everyone had a name. And these names are said to have been given to people by their parents.

I read that in a book.

Maybe a long, long time ago it was really like that.

The names were just like the ones characters in famous novels have, things like Pyotr Verkhovensky and Oliver Twist and Jack Oshinumi.

I bet that was great.

"Prithee, my dear Adrian Leverkühn, whither headest thou?"

"Ain't noneryer business wherah head. Amah mistook, Mori Rintaro?"

These days hardly anyone has a name like that. The only ones who still do are the actresses and the politicians.

Later on everyone started naming themselves. I can recall a bit of that.

People were totally crazy about naming themselves. All the folks who had been given names by their parents would go to City Hall to have their old names swapped for new ones they had thought up themselves.

There was always a long line at City Hall.

The line was so long that if two people became lovers when they first lined up, a newborn baby would be carried off in an ambulance around the time City Hall finally came into view.

Officials chucked tons of old names into the river behind City Hall.

Millions of old names jostled and bobbled over the entire surface of the river, completely obscuring the water. Slowly, quietly, they drifted downstream.

Every day the little tricksters in my gang would gather at the river's edge and have fun chucking rocks at them, yelling and peeing on the old names as they passed.

"Ya-a-a-a-agh
Ya-a-a-a-agh
Stupid nincompoops!!
Ya-a-a-a-agh
Ya-a-a-a-agh
Uvulas!!"

Lined up along the riverbank, we showered abuse upon the stricken, bug-eyed old names; then, in unison, we would whip out our foreskinned weenies.

"Ready! AIM!"

We braced ourselves.

"*FIRE!!*"

The sad old names would writhe in agony beneath the sudden volley of our pee, floundering this way and that, unable to raise a hand against us.

"Shitbrats!
Bedwetters!
Unfilial swine!!"

Trying their best to anger us, the old names drifted off to the sea.

Often the names people chose were kind of strange.

Yeah, there were loads of strange names.

The person who had taken the name and the name the person had taken were constantly getting into fights; sometimes they even killed each other.

It was then that we got used to "Death."

We would shoulder our backpacks, step into our galoshes, and then head off to school, sloshing our way along avenues flooded ankle-high with the blood of people and their names.

Day after day, convoys of eight-ton trucks mounded high with the corpses of people and their "names" sped along the highways.

When I was in third grade, one of my classmates named himself without telling his parents.

"You shouldn't do it," I said.

"Trust me, I can handle it," said the guy.

"My name is really nice," he'd say.

But his "really nice" name ended up killing him.

It was a horrifically gruesome death.

So gruesome no one could believe the body had ever been a person.

2.

At some point we started naming ourselves differently. Two splendid lovers were the first to name themselves the new way. Unfortunately their names haven't been passed down.

The man had no name. He didn't want his parents to name him, and he didn't want to name himself. He was also tired of all the killing. He figured he was getting along just fine without a name.

The woman felt the same way.

There was, however, one drawback to this.

The man kissed the woman's breast, he kissed her thin clavicle and the nape of her neck. Then he tried to whisper his beloved's name into her ear.

"My lovely . . ." he began. Then, bewildered, he paused.

It just didn't feel right.

Putting a temporary halt to their intercourse, the man pulled on his underwear and sat down on the bed.

Hiding her breasts with her hands, the woman rubbed her cheek coyly against the man's as he stared glumly at the ceiling.

"What is it, honey?" asked the woman. "You don't like me anymore?"

"No, it's not that," said the man. "It's just that murmuring 'Oh, my lovely . . .' like that gives me the creeps. It's so abstract, you know, I'm afraid I'll end up impotent."

"Oh honey, you're so sensitive!"

The woman got on all fours on the bed and waited there

for the man to come up with a good solution.

"It's inconvenient not having a name," said the man.

"Yeah. But it wasn't inconvenient until just now, huh?" replied the woman.

It hadn't been at all inconvenient. The two of them had been humping like there was no tomorrow, full of joy.

They gazed fondly at each other's bodies. Until now they had been so busy kissing and closing their eyes and what all that they hadn't had the leisure just to sit back and take a good look at one another.

How subtle these bodies of ours are, the man thought.

"My God, I've done some shockingly lewd things to you, haven't I?" said the man. For some reason, he just felt like saying this.

"Yes you have! Boy, have you ever! Lots and lots and lots! You did loads of lewd things to me!!" replied the woman spiritedly, smooching his cheek.

"I'm afraid I owe you an apology."

"Hey, don't worry about it! Let's face it, you're a hunk!"

According to William of Ockham, people's souls are all structured in the same way: they are spherical in shape with a hollow cavity in the middle; when the archangel Gabriel puts his finger on the surface and makes the sign of the cross, the person trembles and begins chanting, "Glory be unto the name of the Lord!" The couple realized that bodies, on the other hand, are much more intricate and finely tuned.

The man saw now that lovers need names. Not names chosen by their parents, not names they have selected on their own; surely there was a method of naming more appropriate to lovers, the man thought.

"Let's try this," said the man. "You think of a name that fits me and you give it to me. I'll think of a name that's perfect for you and I'll give it to you. We'll have them as names only we can use. How do you like that?"

"Oh, yes, yes! I love it! You're the greatest!"

And so the two christened each other.

The lovers kept the names secret, so we don't know what they were.

The man spoke the woman's name.

The woman spoke the man's name.

"See, it's neither abstract nor common. It couldn't fit your body better," said the man as he slipped off his underwear.

The woman rolled the man's name across her tongue, entranced.

"Now!" hollered the woman, "Get in the mood and let's go!"

3.

And so we began naming each other.

We ask the person we want to name us to give us a name.

It's our method of courting.

I've been given names and then lost them any number of times. I went around without any name at all for quite a while before I met Song Book.

Slowly, through many renamings, we grow cautious.

4.

"I'd like you to give me a name," I told the woman.

"Okay," she replied.

And then—

"You give me a name, too," she added.

"Henry IV" had finished his milk-and-vodka, and was fast asleep in his basket.

We had just made love for the first time, and lay in a cozy embrace.

I went over to my desk and wrote the woman's name on a sheet of paper.

The woman rolled over on the bed so that she faced the other way.

She was scribbling my name in her little notebook.

I gazed at the woman's naked back.

I'd never known a woman's back could be so lovely.

5.

The woman took the paper I'd written her name on and read it.

The Nakajima Miyuki Song Book

"Thank you," said the woman.

6.

There were many poets writing in Japanese late in the 20th century.

We call that period "The Age of the Three Great Poets."

The works of all but the three greatest have been forgotten.

Tanikawa Shuntaro, author of "Watching Her Play in Water," is one.

Tamura Ryuichi, author of "With Rosy Cheeks," is the second.

And Nakajima Miyuki, authoress of "If You Must Sail, Set Sail in September," is the third. This poem appears on the B side of her seventh album.

I've always hoped that the book of poems I'm eventually bound to write will be as dazzling a collection as *The Nakajima Miyuki Song Book*.

"The Nakajima Miyuki Song Book."

This was the woman's name.

7.

I read the note Song Book had written.

Sayonara, Gangsters

"Thank you," I said.

8.

"I used to be a gangster," said Song Book.
"But I'm not a gangster now.
Not anymore," said Song Book.
So "Sayonara, Gangsters" is my name.

II "Stop it, just stop it!"

1.

Once, just once, I met the gangsters.

I was at the bank.

I was sitting on the sofa, reading a newspaper and watching a soap opera.

In the soap opera a couple that was in love at the beginning broke up at the end, and a man and woman who weren't in love at the beginning either fell in love or passed that stage and broke up at the end, and the main character either found or lost himself either in his room or in the park or while sitting at his desk writing a letter, and the pregnant heroine was either sobbing or in a dither or in a slump and either got dumped by the man or dumped the man, and whenever a sexy scene got under way the camera always zoomed in for a close-up shot of a curtain or doorknob in a manner reminiscent of the self-centered delusions of a schizophrenic.

I had just lost my job and my girlfriend. The papers I read and the soap operas I watched as I sat on the sofa in that air-conditioned bank were all I had.

While I was commuting to the bank, half the characters in the soap opera died and the other half either went crazy or became novelists or reached the point where nothing but the socks of grade school girls could turn them on. Calling goodbye to me from beyond the screen, all those characters disappeared.

Three large wars broke out, enough smaller wars started that they'd have spilled from the back of a truck, there was a climax, new sponsors came and went, the enigmatic beauty who had bowled over a million men gazed straight at me and whispered, "If you want to have sex with me, buy this eyeshadow!" and then the new troop of characters arrived.

2.

An old man lived on the bank's sofa. You might say he was its proprietor.

The old man was 91; he'd been coming to the bank every day for 37 years.

"Life was like a dream," he said, gazing at the TV.

The old man didn't watch TV the way I did.

His style of watching TV was unlike anyone else's.

When the actors started yelling and slipping off their panties and doing their best to hotpotato responsibility for the war onto the extortionist shareholder who was scheming to take over the company, the old man would speak to the screen.

"Stop it, just stop it!"

The corrupt, heavy-drinking lawyer who had been shotgunned to death in the old soap opera by the eighth-ranking featherweight of the Far East division (the man was both the boyfriend and, we learn in the last episode, the long-lost big brother of the lawyer's daughter-in-law, whom the lawyer had violated) appeared in the new soap opera in the role of a young brain surgeon who is troubled by nightmares about homosexual experiences he had in his prewar high school days and goes around slicing open the head of anyone he can lay his hands on.

"Stop it, just stop it!"

3.

"Put your hands in the air!" shouted the gangsters.

There were four of them, dressed in recognizable gangster style.

They had on black hats, black three-piece suits, and spotless white gloves, and they held matching machine guns. They stood there with an air of solemn dignity, just like Al Capone or John Dillinger or Clyde Barrow.

"We don't wanna have to get rough!" said the gangsters.

Holding up our hands, fidgeting nervously, we gazed at the gangsters as they carried out their work, doing everything with speed and finesse.

The customers and the clerks and I were all extremely delighted to have been set upon by the celebrated gangsters.

We held our hands up for a while even after they had gone, enjoying the aftermath of the attack.

4.

"Stop it, just stop it!" said the old man.

Even while the gangsters were marauding the bank, terrorizing us all with the threat of death and violence, the old man's eyes remained glued to the screen.

In the soap opera, gangsters were wallowing in a vast sea of blood.

Looking cool, Eliot Ness put his Colt Detective .38 into his satchel.

"So much violence," murmured Eliot Ness.

"Stop it, just stop it!" replied the old man.

5.

I teach poetry at a poetry school.

It makes me feel very odd to say "I teach poetry at a poetry school."

It makes me feel sort of like a bellboy at the old Imperial Hotel in Tokyo trying his best to maintain a posture as stiff as a rod while holding a tray with a chilled beer on it when right next to him Katharine Ross is carefully rinsing out the inner recesses of her vagina with her portable bidet.

6.

I'm sure it also feels odd to be told that "I teach poetry at a poetry school."

"You don't say?" people moan, or "Isn't that something!" and then they just stand there, grinning at me, their minds racing as if they're trying to work through the most difficult puzzle in the world.

Lost in their thoughts, they begin to droop.

And so I send out the lifeboat.

"Listen, it's just another job.

I had no choice, you see, I needed a job.

Teaching poetry is no different from typing 60 words a minute or conveying 100 volts of electrical current into the head of a pig and sending it off to heaven, and I don't think I need to feel ashamed of what I do."

"Of course not! It's a great job, really, that teaching poetry stuff! I mean, it's poetry you're talking about, right? Wow, that's *so* incredible!"

They cling ecstatically to the lifeboat I've sent them; they kick the surface of the water with their feet, grabbing onto my boat so unabashedly you'd think it was an inflatable vinyl ring they had brought along themselves.

"And do you teach novels as well?"

I teach poetry at a poetry school.

7.

I've long held that poetry must be charming.
Great poetry has always been charming.
The Book of Ecclesiastes was charming.
The Iliad and *Illuminations* and *Howl* and *Coca-Cola Lessons* and *Sergeant Pepper's Lonely Heart Club Band* were all, each and every one, charming poems.
The Pisan Cantos are the only exception. People can say what they like, they're an exception. They may be great, but as far as I could see there was nothing even remotely charming in them, and so I decided to go out on one of the bi-monthly large-garbage collection days and toss them unobtrusively onto the pile.

8.

" 'Of simple plots and actions the episodic are the worst. I call a plot episodic when there is neither probability nor necessity in the sequence of its episodes. Actions of this sort bad poets construct through their own fault, and good ones on account of the players. His work being for public performance, a good poet often stretches out a plot beyond its capabilities, and is thus obliged to twist the sequence of incident.' "

"Mee-eo-oo-oo-oo-ow-www."

Song Book was sitting in the rocking chair, dressed in a flowing white dress, and "Henry IV" sat purring in her lap. She was reading to him from Aristotle.

Song Book has a voice like a very old monaural recording—made just a short while before the advent of stereo—of Pablo Casals playing his cello.

"Give peace a chance!" said Pablo Casals.

Then he played Bruch's "Kol Nidrei."

Everyone in the audience at the Royal Opera House in Covent Garden wept. The director from EMI who oversaw the recording wept together with the mixer, the producer, and the coordinator; Otto Klemperer, seated down in the pit with his mistress, wept; so did the guards and the lid of the toilet.

I wonder what made them weep.

I wonder why charming sounds make people sad.

" 'The poet being an imitator just like the painter or other maker of likenesses, he must necessarily in all instances represent things in one or other of three aspects, either as they were or are, or as they are said and thought to be or to have been, or as they ought to be.' *Mon chéri*, would you be a dear and run warm up 'Henry IV' 's milk?"

"*Mais oui!*" I said.

"Henry IV" is a great fan of Aristotle. He also likes Kant.

Whenever Song Book is out somewhere and can't read to him, I read the part where Kant demonstrates with equal clarity both that God does and does not exist. "Henry IV" listens, his ears quivering with delight.

9.

"Henry IV" sleeps in his basket in a corner of our bedroom.

When I met Song Book, the basket with "Henry IV" in it was all she had.

" 'Henry IV' was born in this basket, you know. There were six kittens in the litter, but 'Henry IV' was the only one who survived. His mother died, too," said Song Book. "And 'Henry IV' thinks he killed them."

The very first time Song Book kissed me, "Henry IV" was gazing up at us from inside his basket, blinking his eyes.

"Henry IV" is a giant, black, ugly cat who drinks vodka-and-milk cocktails and then falls asleep at our feet.

III "Kiss me"

1.

Song Book takes everything off before she gets into bed.

We must have slept in the same bed at least 100 times, but I always get shy.

The whole time Song Book is removing her dress and panties or stockings I feel so shy, so terribly shy that I just sit in the chair and pray.

It seems the mortification will continue forever, when a ready-as-she'll-ever-be Song Book starts scolding me from the bed like some impatient omnipotent god: "*Mon chéri,*" she says, "what are you doing?!"

At last I take off my clothes.

Song Book ogles me the whole time.

"I love looking at your body," says Song Book.

Feeling shy, feeling so shy, feeling so incredibly shy that I simply can't continue, I ask Song Book if it'd be all right for me to come to bed with my undies on.

"I guess, but you'll be taking them off anyway, right?"

When I get naked, I always feel so naked.

When Song Book gets naked, she still seems to have on one last petticoat.

"That's ridiculous!" says Song Book.

"When I get naked I really get naked, but when you get naked you don't seem to get naked at all," she retorts in her Aristotelian manner.

Thinking about the body is hard.

It's so hard that ultimately even Aristotle threw in the towel.

Song Book's breasts fit the hollows of my palms like a glove. No matter how many times I try putting my hands on them, they still fit just as perfectly.

"No riddles while we're in bed, okay?" Song Book whispers as she reaches over and wraps her hands around mine.

I couldn't agree more.

As far as I'm concerned, beds are meant for making love, for falling asleep in while holding hands, or for flipping over to serve as a barricade, and nothing else.

2.

Song Book is very gentle when she makes love.

It's sad when you're making love and you feel as though your bodies are simply machines for making love.

I feel fulfilled when I'm making love to Song Book.

Making love is a dialogue.

Sometimes even though you're making love it feels as if you're masturbating. That really gets you down.

Song Book has just said something to me.

Song Book wraps her arm around my neck and gives it a tug.

The slope between her jaw and her neck is right before my eyes.

I start feeling like a 57-year-old virgin from India with an empty stomach.

Song Book's body slowly curves into an arc, effortlessly lifting me up.

"Enter me," says Song Book.

3.

I was having a strange dream.

The 100,000 spectators in the grandstand were all on their feet, belting out a chorus of "My Old Kentucky Home" as I galloped past, 14th out of 14 in the race.

Speeding like a bullet into the distance was—

Kentucky Sherry, whose trainer, Alice Richards, had sent him out to the track with the command, "If you're going to die, die in the front!" And rocketing along in third place was my number one rival, Forward Pass.

It was May 4th, 1968, at Louisville's Churchill Downs, and I was Dancer's Image, starting at post position nine, now zipping along the back stretch.

I was clocking 24.14 for the quarter mile.

I kept my eyes fixed on Forward Pass.

I could tell I was going to win.

As we rounded the far turn and barreled into the stretch, the hooves of the horses before me started falling out of rhythm, moving with less snap than before, while I shot ahead on a sudden crest of energy.

Gleaming Sword, Captain's Gig, Don B., Jig Time, T.V. Commercial . . . one by one I blew past the other horses.

Kentucky Sherry fell away behind me, and I overtook Forward Pass.

I'm a horse in the Kentucky Derby!

An eighth of a mile to the finish line.

An unbelievable sight met my eyes.

All of a sudden, Nodouble, Martins, and Yankee Lad were galloping alongside each other so that they formed a barricade in front of me, intentionally blocking my way.

It was the May 18th Preakness at Pimlico, and I was falling into their trap.

I saw Forward Pass thundering ahead on the other side of the three-horse wall, although of course I had already passed him once before.

"Get outta my way!" I screamed.

The three thoroughbreds were goofing off, reeling and skipping and squealing and tripping, doing everything they could to keep me from passing.

"I'll freaking kill you, jerks!" shouted my gangster jockey.

"Oh no, I wouldn't. . ." I stammered.

"Arrgh! I can't stand it!"

Up on my back the gangster began blasting away with his machine gun.

Bounding over the hole-filled corpses of the three dead horses, I streaked like the wind past Forward Pass, who had fled into the stands in his confusion.

I kept running and running down the long, long track.

No matter how far I go, I can't see the finish line.

4.

I was still dreaming.

In my dream I was feeling bewildered because I couldn't figure out what sort of dream I was supposed to be having in the dream.

In the dream, I just kept hoping I would wake up from the dumb dream.

But now that the dream had gotten its hands on me, it simply refused to leave me alone, as if it were a gaggle of reporters and I were the only passenger to emerge alive from the wreckage of a crashed jumbo jet.

"Get your hands off me!" I shouted.

I let the dream have ten seconds. Then, since it still gave no sign that it was inclined to release me, I gave it a brutal kick in what appeared to be its vitals.

"Ungh!" groaned the dream. "Man, you suck."

5.

"What was that, Song Book? Did you say something?"

Her hair and forehead pressed to my chest, Song Book was speaking in her sleep.

"THE GANGSTERS . . . THE GANGSTERS . . ." moaned Song Book.

After that she took a little break.

Then, "THE GANGSTERS . . . THE GANGSTERS . . . THE GANGSTERS . . ."

Song Book's body gets in a weird state when she's having a nightmare.

"It's all right, THE GANGSTERS aren't coming," I said.

I had whispered this into her ear using a very delicate intonation that made it possible for her to hear me even inside her dream.

"It's all right, I'm here," I said. "THE GANGSTERS won't try to come and get you, not as long as I'm here."

Slowly I stroked the tension from Song Book's narrow waist.

Then slowly, slowly, ever so slowly I stroked her back, tracing her deep S-shaped curve with my fingers. Slowly, slowly, ever so slowly I stroked her stomach, which was so soft that when you pressed down on it your fingers just kept sinking in forever.

Song Book's body returned to normal.

Without waking, still fast asleep, Song Book let her eyelids quiver just a little, as if to tell me that everything was all right now; and then she began talking to me from within some other dream.

"Kiss me," said Song Book.

I gave Song Book a kiss.

Asleep in his basket, "Henry IV" rolled over.

He whined quietly, like a sick dog.

Phhuuuuunn.

IV "ЧООЧY"

1.

> Those Who Write Imaginatively
> Must Be Prepared to Face a Firing Squad

This is the poster on the door of "The Poetry School" where I teach.

The famous dictum is short and clear, and it is also true.

2.

My slogans are posted side by side on the lavatory wall at "The Poetry School."

Put Your Piss in the Pot

If you can't get a poem to work
take it down to the blacksmith
and have him smash it to pieces
with his hammer

               -Horace

It is my hope that our students will abide by both slogans.

3.

I've been writing poetry for a long time.

I was three years old when I wrote my first poem: I wrote it with a CRAYON in my mother's household account-book.

I wanted to write a poem praising my beloved plastic duck potty-seat.

The first line of every first poem comes on a wave of inspiration.

I gripped my CRAYON, so tense I was shaking.

I was still unaware of the tenet propounded by poets of the Classical school, who thought all poems should begin either with the name of God or with some name demonstrative of His dignity; I was also unaware of the rebuttal of "d'Alembert's principle" that Valéry had put forth, "the rigorous but just law which our century imposes on poets: it recognizes as good in verse only that which it would find excellent in prose."

I was a three-year-old baby in diapers whose parents kept hoping and hoping that he would stop wetting his bed, before they finally gave up.

Sweeping my hand down across the masses of numbers that buried the pages, with enough energy to send them all toppling, I wrote five enormous letters:

ꟼOOꟼY

I had still only written that one word when my mother

discovered me sitting there in a stupor, clutching my CRAYON.

"It's 'P' not 'Ԁ,' you dolt!" said my mother.

"Didn't I tell you to come and get me when you need to go poopy?" she added. "You're a pathetic excuse for a child!"

Mom, I didn't want to go poopy, I wanted to write a poem.

4.

I wrote and I wrote and I kept on writing.
When I turned seventeen I learned I was a "Poet."
It was "The Hall" who told me that I was a "Poet."

5.

The guy and I had to stand in the hall.

Our history teacher came and stood in front of me.

"So tell me, kid, are you sure the man who discovered America in 1492 was Babe Ruth?" he asked.

"No," I said. "I'm sorry, I had it wrong. It was Marlon Brando."

"Stand here for another hour," said the teacher.

Our history teacher went and stood in front of the guy.

"Do you still think that the name of the drama Shakespeare wrote in 1598 at the behest of Queen Elizabeth I was *Emmanuelle*?" he asked.

"Uhhhhm," moaned the guy. He stood for some time with his arms crossed, deep in thought; then suddenly a winsome grin darted across his face and he whispered something into the teacher's ear.

"Stand here until tomorrow morning!!" said the teacher.

The guy spent the few precious years of that difficult period of life standing in the hall at school.

Like a Jew who has finally found the Promised Land, he never budged an inch from his spot in the hall.

The guy was still standing in the hall the day I graduated. As the teachers and students passed by, he called out cheerfully, "Hey, I'm the hall!"

"Goodbye," I said to him.

It was hard to go off and graduate, leaving him alone there in the hall.

"Oh, I don't mind," said the guy. "You see, I've discovered

that I'm the hall. It's not bad at all being the hall, to tell you the truth. Hey, listen . . . there's something I want to tell you. Speaking as the hall, I mean. You've got what it takes to be a poet, kid, you really do. Hallistically speaking, it's obvious."

Channeling all the strength in my body into my eyes, I stared at the guy.

By then it was practically impossible to distinguish him from the hall, and you had the feeling that if you relaxed your attention even a tiny bit you would no longer be able to locate him.

"You think I have what it takes to be a poet?" I asked.

The guy made a noise like squeaky shoes.

"There are all different kinds of halls!" cried the guy.

Evidently he no longer understood the words I spoke.

"Most halls are straight, but when they turn they turn at right angles.

If you walk down a hall upside-down, people call the place you're walking the ceiling. Which implies that the ceiling is also the hall. It seems likely that if you were to walk on the ceiling your shoes would squeak."

I said goodbye to the squeaking hall.

I had learned that I was a poet.

6.

I've written many poems over the years.

But my poems have always had very few readers. So few it's pathetic.

Until I turned twenty, my poems had only three readers.

One reader was *me*.

I would always read the poems I had written with great care, and then send a fan letter to the author.

> Keep up the good work, and don't let yourself get discouraged. I feel sure something nice will come your way. I give you my word on that.
>
> Isidore Ducasse had only one reader right up until the day he died, and yet he was always just as spunky as Tom Sawyer.
>
> Over the course of history 60% of all poets have had only one reader, and there are tons of poets who were so sickened by the poems they wrote that they would never even dream of reading them. Please do not let it get to you that you don't have many readers. Incidentally, there is one thing that troubled me about your latest poem. Tell me, what exactly is that "condom" supposed to represent? If it's intended as a metaphor for "alienated sex," well, doesn't that seem a trifle too easy?
>
> I hope everything is going well.
>
> Yours truly,
> A Reader

Another reader was my mother.

Every time I wrote a poem and mailed it to her, my mother would send me an envelope of cash by registered mail in return.

My mother interpreted all my poems as requests for money.

The third reader was a man who called himself a poet, who was always saying that poets should never read anything they had written.

The man and I read each other's poems.

I spent a lot of time reading the man's "poems," doing my best to be thorough. But no matter how many times I looked them over, I could never figure out how or where to begin reading.

"You've got to study a lot to understand my poems," the man told me.

I doubted I would understand his "poems" even if I studied a lot.

The "poems" the man wrote were more like some variety of secret code used by a colony of ants that had been exposed to fatal levels of radiation and lost the capacity to reproduce than like any poems I had ever encountered.

"Hey, that's the *back!*" said the man.

He always said this when I started reading his "poems."

There were five ○s and five ×s written on the paper he had handed me, that was all; I had been watching the random scattering of ○s and ×s as they played their soccer match, wondering which team was winning.

"Hey, that's the *back*, too," said the man, his voice full of sadness.

I had just flipped the man's "poem" and started reading it anew.

On the reverse side of the paper there was a green caterpillar, stuck down with cellophane tape. The caterpillar was wiggling its legs around like crazy, howling out in a voice choked with tears that if it had to be turned into a "poem" by the man it would rather just be stepped on and squashed.

Whenever the man saw me reading one of his works in a straight line from top to bottom, or flipping it over and reading the back, or poking a hole in the middle with my finger and reading it that way, or folding it up into a paper airplane and sending it flying, his face took on a look of disappointment and despair.

Since the man wasn't just the author of his "poems," but also one of the precious few readers of my own works, I always did my best to read his literary productions in a way that would make him happy.

The man absolutely refused to entertain questions.

Once I stupidly asked him, "What's the theme of this poem?"

The following was written on the paper he'd handed me:

Hitler was so thrilled with *Gone With the Wind* that he unpacked his secret collection of his mother's old panties and spread them out on bed and fell asleep among them, singing "Twinkle, Twinkle, Little Star."

Seeing that this "poem" was written in words I could understand, I had gotten excited and let myself get a little carried away.

Of course that wasn't a question I should have asked.

The man snatched the paper back from me, then balled it up and swallowed it. He turned his back on me and began striding briskly away.

"Hey! Hey, wait!" I yelled after him.

The man just kept striding away. He halted at a Kentucky Fried Chicken and took up a position alongside the Colonel Sanders mannequin, sticking his hands out in front of him in just the same way.

Colonel Sanders and the man preached *The Gospel of Fried Chicken* to all the ladies and gentlemen walking up and down the street.

"Hey! Hey, come on! I said I'm sorry!" I shouted.

"Sonny, our theme is 27 different kinds of spices!!" Colonel Sanders called out kindly to me in place of the man, who maintained a sullen silence.

7.

The man would gaze blankly for two or three seconds at the poems I wrote, then sniff them and lick them and hold them up to the sun, and then ask me, "Is this part with the writing the whole poem?"

"Yes," I would reply.

"Kind of simple, isn't it?" the man would say.

My poems were kind of simple.

My poems are and will probably continue to be kind of simple.

My poems are kind of simple, just like their author.

8.

All kinds of things happened between then and my days at "The Poetry School," when I met Song Book.

Lots and lots of all kinds of things happened.

The first three years I worked at an illustrious auto factory.

At the auto factory I was given the gift of an enormous burn on my right elbow that will remain with me forever.

I was thinking about how Rimbaud must have felt as he bumped along in his carriage from Paris's Gare de l'Est on the 23rd of August, 1891, when I accidentally shoved my elbow up against an 850°F engine mold.

The next three years I worked at an illustrious iron factory.

This time things worked themselves out the other way: I ended up making the factory a present of the pinky toe of my right foot.

I was working at a 20-ton hammer that slammed down once every 13 seconds and flattened pieces of pig iron, murmuring to myself the words of a poem.

"Eat your pineapple Savor your pheasant
Stupid Stalin Your end is near"

I was just wondering whether Mayakovsky had written those lines or whether, in fact, their author had been Stalin himself when I made the mistake of sticking out a foot along with the next piece of iron.

The last three years, I was an illustrious construction worker. During those three years, I made up my mind never to think about poetry on the job.

Even so I ended up falling from an 18-foot scaffold.

I emerged from all this with a big ugly scar on my right elbow, no pinky toe on my right foot, and a limp, but I was still a poet.

9.

Suitably enormous conveyor belts flowed through that illustrious auto factory. We called the conveyor belts "lines."

Everything imaginable flowed past us, riding its "line."

One "line" flowed past carrying sand destined to be made into molds for four-cylinder engines.

One "line" flowed past carrying chassis.

One "line" flowed past carrying shafts.

One "line" flowed past carrying windshield wipers.

One "line" flowed past carrying tachometers.

One "line" flowed past carrying clutch disks.

One "line" flowed past at a high speed carrying a "line" that carried pamphlets warning that you mustn't forget to squirt oil once every four months around the rotating rod and a "line" warning that you musn't forget to check the fourth screw from the right on the frame of the windshield.

One "line" flowed past carrying the section chief who poked me in the ribs as I sat scrutinizing a "line" that carried a "line" that carried a "line" that carried some sort of object that I just couldn't figure out.

I'm sure Heraclitus, who said "All is flux," worked in the illustrious auto factory, he must have.

Three rotating shifts flowed past on its "line."

The head nodding off beneath the body-presser during the break from one to two AM gets lopped off along with its *23 Years of Service!* hat on the signal GO! flowed past on its "line."

Poorly understood, it all just kept flowing past.

"Poorly understood, it all just kept flowing past" just kept flowing past.

Kept flowing past.

"All you things that keep flowing past me

Where do you come from

And where do you think you're going?" I'd ask, but the 72 types of hardtops in 24 colors and the members of the House of Councillors and the 18 different choices of set menus and the 64 different wage levels based on performance just kept on flowing past.

"Keep flowing, 'line'!

Even after

The universe perishes

You will flow on."

10.

Even then the gangsters were famous.

Every day articles about the gangsters appeared in the newspapers.

The Wall Street Journal reported that "Each gangster makes off with $100 million annually from organizations around the world."

The gangsters released a statement saying, "Unfortunately, the inflation rate makes an annual decrease in revenue of eight percent unavoidable."

When the nine-minute break we had every 125 minutes started, we'd take a seat on the break time that came flowing along on its "line" and chat about the gangsters.

"What kind of 'line' do you think the gangsters are on?" we would ask.

"What kind of 'line' do you think the gangsters are on?" flowed from where we sat chatting toward the next "line" at a velocity of three inches per second.

11.

I was living then with a young, healthy woman.

I don't really remember what I called her.

I was always getting the woman's name mixed up with the names of various characters who appeared in the "poems" I wrote.

Of course, the woman was constantly mixing up my name with the names of the lover she had had before me and the lover she had had before the lover she had had before me and the lover she had had before the lover she had had before the lover she had had before me, so in the final analysis it was tit-for-tat.

I called the woman *my little 'Rabbit'* and *my little 'Strawberry'* and *my little 'Kitten'* and *my little 'Meg the Witch'* and *my little 'San Francisco Giants Relief Ace.'*

She called me by lots and lots of names.

12.

The woman looked at me and murmured, "Oh, my little 'riverrun brings us by a commodious vicus of recirculation back to Howth Castle and Environs.'"

I was just about to ejaculate, so I couldn't help being annoyed.

After kissing the tip of the woman's slightly sweaty nose, I urged her to be more careful.

"You see, 'riverrun brings us by a commodious vicus' isn't my name."

"Oh yes, *mais oui*, you're so completely right, my little 'riverrun, past Eve and Adam's, from swerve of shore to bend of Dublin's bay to the forest by the road that leads to the graveyard, vanishing with each step ahead: we will always be the Wife and Husband stars inside the Milky Way,' oh yes, *tu as raison*."

Smacking the woman's lovely bottom, I shouted the woman's names.

"My little 'Rabbit!'

My little 'Strawberry!'

My little 'Kitten!'

My little 'Meg the Witch!'

My little 'San Francisco Giants Relief Ace!' Hup hup, you're up!

Vida Blue gave up four balls to a string of six batters starting with the first to step up to the plate, and no sooner had he slammed that fatal fork ball of his into the helmet of batter number seven than he went and committed harakiri on the mound! Relief! Relief! Get out there!"

"Houm?" said the woman. "What's up with you?"

"Please don't call me by other people's names when we're having sex," I said.

I was always saying this.

Because it's such a delicate moment.

"I'm sorry, I'm sorry," said the woman.

Then:

"I'm sorry, I'm sorry, I'm sorry, I'm sorry, I'm sorry. I'm sorry, I'm sorry, I'm sorry, I'm sorry, I'm sorry," said the woman. And then as an extra special bonus, just for me, she added "I'm sorry!" with a sheepish smile.

"No problem," I said. "Don't let it get to you."

By then it no longer seemed to matter so much whether the woman had been calling me by another man's name.

No matter what facts emerged to try and prevent me from loving the woman, I still loved her.

We picked up where we had left off, just before ejaculation.

"I'm sorry, I'm sorry, I'm sorry, I'm sorry," chanted the woman.

As I came, the woman yelled yet another another man's name.

But why should I let that bother me?

The woman and I clung tightly, tightly, tightly to each other's dying bodies, practically shouting that our undying spirits could eat shit and die.

"Oh, that was wonderful, my little

'As Gogol died he cried out: The ladder, the ladder—
Maupassant said: It's dark, it's dark—
Byron cried: Go on, go on—
All three of these men bequeathed unto us
Such suggestive last words
Tell me folks, which do you like best
Personally I like Byron's best of the three.
When they shot Muto Sanji he yelled as he fell:
A matter for the crematory!' that was wonderful sex," the
woman said
    to me.

13.

I worked at an illustrious iron factory.

At the illustrious factory, "Earplugs" symbolized life and prosperity.

BamBamBaHeybuddy!**mBamBamB**Huhh?Whadd ayaawann?**amCRASHCRASHCRASHCRA**Gimmet h**SHCRA**ebladeforthegrin**SH** ^{POKPOKPOKPOK}_{DUNDUNDUNDUN} derwillyaaa? ^{POKPOK}_{DUNDUN} Hm?Whadayawan? ^{POK}_{DUN} Grinder!**WEEEEEEEEE EE**Whadayawan?**EEEEEEEEEEEG**!R!I!N!**EEEENNN** D!E!R!!!**WRRCHTBAGUMP—WRRCHTBAGUMP—** WR**Whadayawan?**RCHTBAGUMP—WRRCHTBAGUMP** **HOWL**Theblade!Shit!**THEBLADE!!LLLLLLLLLLIN**Who'sb eenhit?Huhhh?Whadaywan?**GHOWLLL**THEG!R!I!**LLLL IN**!D!**NNN**E!R!!IsaidtheGRINDERG ^{ZIPZIP}_{ZAPZAP} — >> **PHT** >> **PHT** >> **PHT** >> **PHT**whadayawan? ^{PHT}_{PHT} >> ^{PHT}_{PHT} >> ^{PHT}_{PHT} >>Dro pdead!Cockfiddler!**SHAARR**I'llgetyoulater!!**RAAAMMNN**

It's said that workers who remove their "Earplugs" at the illustrious iron factory obtain a glimpse of blissful paradise.

Every year an average of 5.4 workers take their leave of the special article in the employment agreement they sign with the illustrious iron factory that reads, "The Company may decline to provide workman's compensation to the Employee in the event that he or she should remove the 'Earplugs' from his or her ears while engaged in the performance of his or her duties." Bravely, the workers take out their "Earplugs."

Their faces radiant with joy, the workers at the illustrious iron factory vanish, gently, into "The Millennial Bliss."

14.

I worked and I wrote poems.

The woman sat through my readings without so much as a grimace.

My poems were nothing at all like the poems other, illustrious poets had crafted, but even so she would listen to me read my poems.

"Oh that's great, that's so great!" she would say. "I think it's great!"

My poems were never about "Love" or "Destiny" or "Alchemy" or "Myth." They were about "regulator bulbs" and "BOTH Brand Concrete Bond Breaker" and "double-framed floors" and "Overtime work merits 25% over base compensation, night work merits 30% over base compensation" and "air compressors" and "φ 40 ferro-concrete masonry" and "suspension permit" and "four-way reinforcement" and "rejected washers" and "copulation."

15.

When I got home from work the woman would come join me in the bath, and she would wash and rinse my hair for me.

She prepared meals for me.

She made coffee for me.

And then I might read her, for example, my poem about the father of all "lines," the "King of the Lines," who lived in the area marked "Do Not Enter" all the way back in the deepest depths of the illustrious factory.

I read to her of the sadness that filled the days of the "King of the Lines," who was so old and senile that he didn't even know he was a "line," and believed he was the descendant of an exalted prince born of an affair between Louis XIV and the Prussian ambassador's elegant wife.

Then the woman and I would get into bed and make love.

Again and again she and I made love. Again and again and again and again she and I would make love.

Over and over and over and over and over.

V "Agathe Just Loves that Frégate"

1.

The woman gave birth to a baby.

When I got home from work, the woman came out of her room with the baby in her arms.

"What's up with the baby?" I asked.

"I gave birth to her," said the woman. "She's yours."

I hadn't even known the woman was pregnant. As a matter of fact, even the woman hadn't known she was pregnant.

"Bet that was a surprise!" I said.

"Yeah, no kidding. But she's so adorable, this baby of ours, she really is. I bet she'll be even more of a beauty than I am," said the woman.

The baby smiled when she saw my face.

"Kyerk kyerk," said the baby.

I took the baby from the woman and held her. It was the first time I had ever held a baby of my own. She was light and warm, and she smelled really nice, and she kept squirming around in my hands.

"Hello," I said to the baby. "I'm your *pater*. Is it okay if I call you 'Caraway'? Will that be all right with you, little baby 'Caraway'?"

"Paaaa," replied Caraway.

"She says she just loves the name 'Caraway,'" I said to the woman.

"No way! She's our little 'Green Pinky.' Isn't that right, coochy-coo? Isn't that right, little 'Green Pinky' darling?"

"Paaaa," replied our little 'Green Pinky.'

2.

Caraway was our treasure.

I wrote poems about Caraway.

I wrote about "nursing baby every three hours" and "baby burping after she drinks her milk" and "Burger's Liver Paste" and "milk bottles with holes of several different sizes" and "gradually poop begins to stink like an adult's" and "three vaccines in one" and "how the expression on baby's face evolves little by little as it moves through the same cycles of ugliness and cuteness" and "be sure to keep the temperature of the bathwater precisely at 104°F" and "Siccarol Baby Powder" and "Peachleaf Cream" and "the first two teeth to come in are on the bottom" and "the speed baby makes as she crawls across the floor, swinging her arms around like oars." I kept writing poems until finally our crap-spurting little angel saw that all was not good and started howling for me to hurry and change her diaper.

3.

Instead of reading Sandburg and Laforgue, I read Piaget and Saito Kihaku and Krupskaya and Matsuda Michio and R.D. Laing and Proudhon and Hagio Moto.

And I learned that if I wanted Caraway to grow up to be a marvelous young woman, there were at least three things I had to teach her before she turned six.

☞ Dancing
☞ Arithmetic
☞ Tongue-Twisters

4.

"All right Caraway, now dance!" I say.

Caraway is in her pajamas; her hair hangs down to her shoulders.

She prances about on the bed.

And I'm the disc jockey.

Caraway dances the blues to Lynyrd Skynyrd's "Tuesday's Gone."

"Hey Pater, am I super?" cries Caraway, trampolining on the bed.

"You sure are! Super-duper!"

Caraway can swing along to any sort of song.

Caraway sways stylishly to Helen Reddy's "You'd Be So Nice to Come Home To."

Caraway dances dynamically to Ella Fitzgerald's "Mack the Knife."

Caraway dances matter-of-factly to Bach's *Inventions for Two and Three Voices,* performed by Glenn Gould. Ignoring Gould's moaning.

Caraway even manages to dance to Albert Ayler's "Bells," which is the sort of piece you'd think no one could ever dance to.

Soaked in sweat, Caraway squats down on the bed.

"Pater! One more song!"

5.

"So Caraway, what's one plus one?" I say.
Caraway nibbles the butt of the pencil she's holding.
"Caraway, don't chew your pencil!"
Caraway unfurls her tongue.
"Uhhhmmm, there are lots of different one plus ones.

Uhhhmmm, if one is Pater and the other one is Mater then there's Pater and there's Mater and then after a while there's Caraway, and Pater and Mater and Caraway are three people, so one plus one yields a grand total of three.

Uhhhmmm, if one is Joseph and the other one is the Holy Virgin Mary then Jesus is born unto the world and Jesus can't be counted so I really have no idea what kind of a sum one plus one produces.

Uhhhmmm, uhhhmmm, Pater? Caraway's confused!"

6.

"Peter Piper picked a peck of pickled peppers.
All right, take it away, Caraway!"
"Peter Piper picked a peck of pickled peppers.
That was eeeeeasy, Pater."
"She sells sea shells by the sea shore! Go for it, Caraway!"
"She sells sea shells by the sea shore! Huh?
That one was even eeeeeasier!! C'mon, Pater!"
"Okay then, how about this one?
If anyone is me then I'm not me
But if I'm me then no one is me
If no one is me then who can I be
If I'm anyone then surely I'm me.
All right Caraway, take it away!"
"Huh? Huh? What was that? Aww, that's sneaky! That's
too hard for me, Pater, Caraway doesn't understand that one
at all! Awwwww! Caraway is just a squirty little half-pint,
she can't understand that one at all!!"

7.

Caraway has terrible manners.

She can't even sit still for the few moments after she finishes off her soup and before the woman brings out the pork chops. She tick-tick-ticks with her fork in 7/8 time and clonk-clonk-clonks with her knife in 3/16 time, and since her little feet don't reach the floor she whacks away at the legs of the chair and the table in a 3/4 time bump-bump-bump waltz and bonk-bonk-bonk bolero, respectively. All of this is, of course, performed simultaneously.

"Tick-tick-tick, clonk-clonk-clonk, bump-bump-bump, bonk-bonk-bonk."

"Be quiet, Caraway!"

"Okay Pater!"

A three-second fermata. Then once again—

"Tick-tick-tick, clonk-clonk-clonk, bump-bump-bump, bonk-bonk-bonk."

Caraway farts.

I'm reading *The 120 Days of Sodom*, and Caraway is sitting on my lap reading *Go Pirates, Go!* She farts when she laughs.

"Caraway! Ladies are not supposed to fart."

"But Mater says it's bad for you to hold farts in."

Caraway tries to pee standing up like me and fails: her underwear and woolen tights and skirt all end up drenched.

"Don't cry, Caraway. Here, let me wipe your nose. Blow."

Caraway sits down at her mother's three-way mirror and starts giving herself a furtive makeover. She puts on lipstick, and her lips expand to three times their size. She swabs a giant ring of eyeliner around each of her eyes, making herself look like a panda done up for its funeral. She pulls on a babydoll nightgown that she's managed to excavate from the woman's dresser, pulling it on over her head. She takes the 20 milliliter bottle of Imprévue that the woman prizes so highly and gobs it on over her head like French dressing.

"Pater! Hey, Pater! Look at me!"

For a moment I just gape, uncertain whether this thing I see standing in front of me is my little daughter or Salvador Dali's *Premonition of Civil War*.

8.

A postcard with a black border arrived.

The postcard had been sent by City Hall. It read: **"We Were So Sorry to Learn of the Death of Your Daughter."**

"What's wrong, Pater?" asked Caraway.

Caraway and I had been playing gangsters.

I was the sniveling policeman. I must have been blown away fifty times with the toy machine gun Caraway toted as part of her gangster getup.

"Please, Ms. Gangster! Ms. Gangster! Spare my life!"

"You're lucky I'm a gentleman, you little punk. I'll give you enough time to say your prayers. But get a move on, I've got work to do!"

"Pater?"

"Don't worry, darling, it's nothing," I said.

"It's all right, Caraway, let's keep playing," I said.

Still toting her machine gun, Caraway flicked her hat back from where it had fallen, letting me see her face, and gazed up at me.

9.

City Hall knows the precise date when each of us will die, and sends out postcards to inform us when the day comes.

The postcards are mailed directly to people over twenty, and to the guardians of people who are under twenty or have been judged incapable of managing their own affairs.

I received the postcard in the morning.

Caraway would die tonight.

10.

I showed the woman the postcard.

"Oh no, our little 'Green Pinky' is . . ." said the woman.

That was all the woman said.

The woman turned, walked into her room, and locked the door from inside.

The woman called out through the door.

"Don't bring 'Green Pinky' to me, I won't see her."

11.

Caraway and I set out on a walk.

I helped Caraway put on a dress with a design of elves drifting slowly down from the sky, coming to pick strawberries from the strawberry field that covered the dress. I had originally planned to give her the dress as a present on her fifth birthday, but now that would be too late.

I fastened a small red ribbon to the shoulder of the dress. This is the sign we use to identify children who are scheduled to die within the day.

Like all children of that era, Caraway understood death.

Most little girls Caraway's age would get scared anyway, and they would cry and have tantrums and stuff when you tried to give them their ribbons.

Caraway didn't say a word.

"Okay, Caraway, let's go," I said.

"What about Mater?" said Caraway.

"Mater says she's not feeling well."

"Oh."

Caraway and I walked, holding hands. There was hardly anyone around in the park, and few people on the walkways. A whole lot of people must be dying today, I thought.

Caraway and I went to the amusement park.

When the ticket collector saw Caraway's ribbon, he gave her a bag of popcorn and a balloon, telling us it was free.

"Thank you," said Caraway.

Two brothers, who looked about eight or nine, both

wearing red ribbons like Caraway's, were playing catch in front of "Showboat Hall."

"Hey!" one of the boys called to Caraway. "You wanna play catch?"

"It's okay, you can go play if you want to," I said.

Caraway walked off toward the boys.

"I've never played catch," she said. "I don't know how."

"It's easy. Here, we'll teach you."

I sat down on a bench.

There was an old man sitting on the bench, too. I figured he had probably brought the boys, he was probably their grandfather or something.

The old man sat stiller than a corpse, not even blinking.

Caraway and the boys played catch for ages.

12.

Though evening fell and the time came for Caraway and I to head home, the boys kept playing catch, and the old man remained seated on the bench.

"*Au revoir,*" said Caraway.

"*Au revoir,* Caraway," said one of the boys.

"*Au revoir,* little 'Green Pinky,' " said the other boy.

Caraway and I held hands as we walked home.

"Hey Pater!"

"What?"

"I can throw a curve ball."

"Wow, that's amazing."

"I can also throw a slider."

"Wow, that's amazing."

"Pater!"

"What is it, Caraway?"

"One of those boys held my hand."

"Quite the mankiller, huh, Caraway?"

"Nah, I wouldn't go that far."

When we got home Caraway and I had a bath. I washed her hair first, then her body. Her hair was light and soft. Her pint-sized body was extremely thin. Her arms especially.

Caraway put on her pajamas, then came to sleep with me in my bed.

"I wish Mater were with us," said Caraway.

13.

Caraway died very quietly.

Resting her head on my arm, she drifted almost immediately into a deep and peaceful sleep. Little by little, bit by bit, her breath weakened.

Then she stopped breathing.

Even lying there with her, I didn't know exactly when she died.

I just kept lying there, not moving.

All of a sudden Caraway spoke.

"Caraway doesn't ever play *pranks*."

I lay there without moving.

She didn't say another word all night.

14.

Morning came and still the woman remained in her room.

There was a phone call from City Hall.

"What time should we send 'The Wagon' around, sir?" they asked.

"The Wagon" is the vehicle that City Hall sends around to collect the bodies of children under the age of ten. One priest and one philosopher always ride along in "The Wagon." It is their job to talk things through with the devastated parents, to help the bereaved come to terms with their loss, so that the bodies can be collected and removed with the greatest possible speed.

"Don't bother," I replied. "I'll take my daughter myself."

"Be sure to take the route designated by the police," said the phone.

15.

I dressed Caraway's corpse in a pair of Levis for Kids overalls and a T-shirt featuring "The Roadrunner and Wile E. Coyote" from the Hanna-Barbera cartoon. It had been her favorite shirt. Then I put her in one of those baskets that you carry over your shoulders and shouldered her.

Her body was heavier than it had been when she was alive.

16.

I followed the route specially designated by the police as the path to be taken by "Guardians Carrying Their Children's Corpses."

It was a swervily curving concrete road, flanked on both sides by a high wall that made it impossible to see in.

There are 27,660 places in town near which people are absolutely forbidden to bring dead bodies. I was only two miles away from "The Children's Graveyard," but in order to reach it I would have to walk 20 miles of swervily curvily swerving curving swerves and curves.

I walked.

17.

"Pater?" called Caraway from the basket on my back.

"What is it, Caraway? Are you thirsty?"

"No, I'm not thirsty, Pater. I want to walk by myself."

"Don't be silly. I like carrying you like this."

The corpses of children are so heavy that in the end some parents make theirs get down and walk at least a portion of the way.

They should just let "The Wagon" come pick up the body, if they're going to end up making the kid walk.

18.

A woman sat on one of the benches.

There was a bench every quarter mile.

There were little roofs over the benches; all they needed were signs in front of them and they would've looked exactly like bus stops.

The woman had on a maternity dress, and she didn't look very pretty, and she didn't look very young, and she didn't look very happy. She looked like she was really tired of sitting there on the bench.

"Howdy!" I said.

The woman shrugged her left shoulder slightly, proving that she wasn't dead.

There was a baby carriage. Inside the carriage lay a baby so desiccated that it had turned into something closely resembling a mummy.

She would be fined if the police found her.

"Well, I'll be off then," I said.

The woman shrugged her right shoulder slightly, signaling to me that I was free to do as I pleased.

When I had taken a few steps, the woman called to me from her bench.

"You're better off as a gangster!"

When I arrived at the next bench I turned to look back at the woman, now a quarter of a mile behind me.

She was still sitting on her bench.

19.

"The Children's Graveyard" is behind City Hall.

The building was designed by a famous architect in a famous architectural style, and the interior was done by a famous painter based on the famous design "Seventh Heaven for Children." An elegy by a famous composer, playing on an endless loop, echoes through the halls.

I presented the "Death Certificate" and our "Identity Papers" in the lobby.

The young woman at the reception desk was about eighteen or nineteen, and she had her hair in a ponytail, and she was very cute.

A lotus-shaped badge affixed to the young woman's formidably developped bosom boasted the motto of "The Children's Graveyard" Section.

The young woman had a blanket draped over her knees.

She'd been reading Warren Beatty's autobiography when I walked in.

"It's really interesting," she said. "Have you read it?"

"A while ago," I told her.

20.

Warren Beatty wrote the book in question at the very end of his life, during the period he spent as a patient at the Sharanton Mental Institution, and it was full of curses and maledictions directed at the Hollywood that had banished him.

"It is just a total lie that I demanded that Arthur Penn change the line 'I've read Dostoyevski's *Crime and Punishment'* because at the time I had only gotten through two thirds of the book.

What I told him was that I hadn't read through to the end because by the time I finished the first two thirds, I'd already figured out the culprit.

Razumihin is the one who bumped off the old lady, you see—Raskólnikov is just protecting him. Razumihin is one of Svidrigaïlov's henchmen. Now, when Sonia finds out about that, she shoots Svidrigaïlov, staging it so that it looks like a suicide. In the beginning I thought that Porfíry had done it, but then it occurred to me that I was reading too much into things."

21.

"Her name is Caraway," I said.

"I understand how you feel," said the young woman.

She kept filling in the blanks on the form as she spoke. Her eyes were golden.

Lately it's chic to color your eyes.

"This is a public record. I can't fill in a pet name."

"I called her Caraway.

The woman called her our little 'Green Pinky.' That's how she's named."

"I don't mean to be offensive, but doesn't it seem a little sentimental to get so hung up on a name? I mean, now that she's deceased and everything."

"You don't think names are necessary?"

"Oh no, I wouldn't say that. It feels great to be called by a name, it really does, especially when the name suits me.

My boyfriend calls me his little 'Boobs' and his little 'Hot Hipster' and his little 'Adorable Crack' and his little 'Blood-curdlingly Sweet-Smelling Pussy' and his little 'Raison/Proof d'/of Etre/Being' and all sorts of other names like that, depending on how he feels at the time.

When my boyfriend and I are making out, you know, and just as I'm about to come, he calls me his little 'Agathe Just Loves that Frégate' or his little 'The Young Woman Ran. The Young Woman Fell. The Young Woman Wasn't Wearing Any Panties' or something like that—man oh man, I feel as if I'm about to come all the way to my *cuticles*.

I think it's boring to go around with only one name.

But you know what? I would not be pleased if someone were to call me their little 'Half-Rotted Slacker' when I died, I really wouldn't."

22.

"Agathe" and "Frégate" rhyme beautifully.

And the young woman and her boyfriend talk about the cutest child brought in that day as they "Agathe Just Loves that Frégate."

Isn't that awful, Caraway?

23.

Inside "The Children's Graveyard," the shelves for the corpses just keep going and going. It's like a library.

Still piggybacking Caraway, I followed the young woman.

Busily jangling her ring of keys, the young woman slid a metal case out from one of the shelves. It looked like one of those boxes people store files in.

"The inside is lined with cork, and they've put urethane padding on top of that. It's quite comfortable, as a matter of fact," said the young woman.

I lowered Caraway into the case.

Caraway's body had stiffened, and I couldn't fit it into the drawer very well. The young woman massaged the body very gently until it softened, and Caraway settled down into the drawer as neatly as could be.

"I'm going to close it now," said the young woman.

Then she pushed the case back into place.

"Is it okay if I stay here?" I asked.

"Sure. We close at eight. Take your time."

The young woman headed back to her seat at the reception desk, swinging her killer body this way and that with evident pride. The uniform hugged her figure tightly, delineating each and every curve as she walked away.

24.

I stood very still in front of Caraway's case.
Stood very still.
Caraway called out to me from her drawer.
"Pater? Are you there?"
"I'm here, Caraway."
"You can go home now, Pater."
I stood very still.

Time passed and kept passing.
Then the closing bell rang.
"Pater."
The voice didn't sound like Caraway's. It was an old lady's voice.
It sounded like she was talking to herself, not to me.
"My little pinky, it's turned green."

25.

"It's because I played pranks."

26.

The young woman at reception had her hands spread on the reception desk. The man behind her had wrapped himself around her large bottom.

The buttons at the front of the young woman's uniform were undone, she had her pants and panties pulled down, and she seemed very lighthearted, and she appeared to be having a lot of fun.

The man still had on his jeans and his T-shirt. He had just unzipped his pants. He, too, seemed lighthearted, and appeared to be having a lot of fun.

The two of them really threw themselves into their sex.

"Ah, my little 'Curlywurly Pubic Hair Cutie,' " said the man, combing the young woman's pubic hair with his fingers, maneuvering his fingers like a brush.

"Mmm!" said the young woman.

"My little 'Salami-Eating Lovely.' "

"My little 'Hard-as-a-Rock Clitoris Darling.' "

Said the man.

" 'Philanderer.' 'Pervert,' " said the young woman.

"My little 'Love-to-Suck Ducky.' "

" 'Deflowering Demon!' "

"My little 'Can't-Get-Enough Sweetie.' "

" 'Vaginal Violator!' 'Aficionado of Abnormal Acts!' "

"My little 'Coitus-Crazed Charmer.' "

" 'Lecherous Old Goat!' 'Peeping Tom!' "

"Ah, 'Mother Dearest.' "

" 'Mobster!' 'Gangster!' 'Your Machine Gun!' "

The young woman noticed me.

"You can go out, it's open," she said, pointing to the exit.

Then she winked at me.

"Sayonara," said the man.

He was clasping the bluishly veiny breasts of the young woman.

I went outside. As I closed the door, I heard the man shout out cheerily—

" 'Agathe Just Loves that Frégate!' "

27.

It was almost dawn. The woman and I lay in bed, asleep.

I was having a considerably erotic dream. Since Caraway died, the woman and I found it unpleasant even to touch each other's bodies.

I woke up feeling unpleasant.

The woman was just getting out of bed.

"What are you doing?"

"I'm going to look for our little 'Green Pinky.'"

"Oh."

"Come help me."

"Okay."

I got out of bed, too.

The woman and I looked here and there, all around the room.

"Darling, could you go look outside?" called the woman as she crept across the tiled floor of the bathroom.

I circled the house three times, then went back to our room.

The woman was flipping the pages of all the books on the shelf, looking.

"Why don't we wait and look again tomorrow," I said.

"All right," replied the woman.

28.

It was almost dawn. The woman and I lay in bed, asleep. I was just sleeping, that was it. No dreams.

The woman was just getting out of bed.

"What are you doing?"

"I'm going to look for our little 'Green Pinky.' "

"Oh."

"Come help me."

"Give me a minute, okay?"

I was extremely tired.

As soon as she was out of bed, the woman started looking for our little "Green Pinky," by herself this time. In the bathroom. In the kitchen. Inside the toilet, behind the television. In the umbrella stand. Under the vase.

The woman went outside.

I listened dreamily as her footsteps faded.

Give me a minute, okay? I'll come help you look when I get up.

The woman never returned.

Part Two
The Poetry School

I "Who's afraid of vampires?"

1.

People who have been suffering for a very long time tend to become malicious. Of course there are also people who suffer but don't become malicious. It must be because something goes wrong with their heads. Like in my case.

It was raining terribly hard.

Over where we left the garbage for pickup, just under the "Incombustibles on Tuesday" poster, sat a polyethylene bucket, a young woman, and another polyethylene bucket.

The polyethylene buckets and the young woman were drenched.

I held my umbrella out over the young woman.

"Actually, it's against the rules to dump people here," I said.

The young woman had nothing on but a flimsy T-shirt and a pair of jeans, and she was shivering from the cold. The young woman looked at me. The young woman found me suspicious.

"Mrkrgnao!" meowed the young woman suddenly.

"Woof woof!" I barked back.

"I majored in French literature in college," she said. "Proust."

"I majored in Russian literature in college," I said. "Dostoyevski."

"I lied. I dropped out of high school and danced in a cabaret, actually."

"I lied, too. I dropped out of junior high and just lazed about doing nothing while my girlfriend worked as a hostess at a cabaret."

"I lied. Actually I studied bullfighting in France, at the Sorbonne."

"Really? You know, that's funny, because I was enrolled in the Pro-Wrestling Department at Columbia University."

"My dad is a detective and my mom is an arbitrator in a family court and my older brother serves in the navy."

"Yow, I'd better watch out then. My father is a pickpocket and my mother is an alcoholic and my older brother works as a con man."

"My grandfather is an Eskimo and my grandmother is a Papuan."

"Is that so? My grandfather is a pygmy and I'm told my grandmother wasn't even human."

"I have eight children."

"Can't compete with you there. I've got three children, three grandchildren, and one great-grandchild. That only makes seven."

"Listen, I think you should know that I'm a sexually frigid lesbian. I've been this way ever since my mother took our pet Saint Bernard as a lover."

"No way, I'm just the same! I've been an impotent homosexual ever since the pencil sharpener I'd been using since elementary school broke!"

The young woman stood up, smiling.

"I only have one breast."

"My neck grows much longer at night, but I try not to let it bother me. I find it's best not to let such things bother you."

"I'm actually starving," said the young woman. "I haven't had anything to eat in ages. Oh god, my head is spinning like crazy!"

I hoisted the nearly-starved-to-death young woman up onto my back.

The young woman was holding a basket.

"What's in there?"

" 'Henry IV,' " said the young woman.

That was how Song Book and I met.

2.

"The Poetry School" is located in the second basement level of a building with seven floors above ground and two below.

The first, second, and third floors of the building are occupied by the largest supermarket in the world, which sells everything.

Yesterday, after my classes were over, I lined up at the register with ten cans of catfood and one three-pound can of MJB Coffee in my shopping basket. I was just behind a Cambodian who was buying a pair of "Prime Ministers," a pair of "Ministers of Defense," and a pair of "Ambassadors to the United Nations." They were on sale: three for the price of two.

I gazed at the total as the clerk punched in the prices, utterly intrigued. The sum ended up being much lower than I had imagined.

The two "Prime Ministers," the two "Ministers of Defense," and the two "Ambassadors to the United Nations" sat huddled in the shopping basket with their knees bent, looking kind of dispirited.

"Man, I don't wanna go to Cambodia," said one "Prime Minister."

"I wouldn't mind Finland or Fiji, some place like that, but Cambodia!" replied the other "Prime Minister."

"Is war big in Cambodia?" asked one "Minister of Defense."

"To be honest, I didn't even realize there were any Cambodians left," answered the second "Minister of Defense."

"Cambodia—that's next to Ethiopia, no?" said one "Ambassador to the United Nations."

"Mommy! Mommy!" wailed the other "Ambassador to the United Nations."

3.

On the fourth floor there's a cabaret, and on the fifth is a sex parlor.

I love hearing about the things that go on up there.

Up there, they play *Letter to the Corinthians* on the radio every day.

The next floor up, the sixth floor, is the place I really love.

A huge river flows on the sixth floor.

The river is *really* huge: I would estimate that it must be at least an eighth of a mile across at its widest point. Even so, except right out in the middle, the water hardly gets any higher than the chin of a third grade girl.

People say the river flows on forever.

Song Book and I head up to have a picnic on the riverbank, taking along one basket containing our lunch and one containing "Henry IV."

We go right up to the very edge of the river and spread our blanket there. Then we set out the tuna sandwiches, the onion-grass salad, and the Morocco Surprise that Song Book has prepared. Morocco Surprise, that's a dessert made from peppercorn, nutmeg, cinnamon, coriander, dried figs, honey, orange peel, and a host of other good things. "Henry IV" and I gobble it down like horses.

Next comes a bottle of lemon wine, a bottle of strawberry wine, a bottle of beer, and a vodka-and-milk cocktail for "Henry IV."

Also for "Henry IV": Sandburg's 36th and 37th definitions of poetry.

"36. Poetry is the achievement of the synthesis of hyacinths and biscuits.

37. Poetry is a mystic, sensuous mathematics of fire, smoke-stacks, waffles, pansies, people, and purple sunsets.

How's it taste? You like it?"

"Meogh meogh meogh" replies "Henry IV." He's feeling terrific.

Song Book and I take off our sandals and sit with our bare feet sunk up to our ankles in the river. The water feels cool on our skin. "Henry IV" rests his chin on the rim of his basket and gazes downstream.

The sunlight is clear and bright and nearly weightless. The light here weighs much less than the light outside, so it never gets on your nerves at all, no matter how brightly it shines. The only problem is that whenever a strong wind blows up, the sunlight gets swept away and it gets a little dark.

Song Book rests her head on my shoulder.

Hardly a word passes between us.

"Henry IV" doesn't speak, either.

After all, this river isn't meant for talking.

I think about the dead. Later on, after we've gone back downstairs, I'll have time to think about the living, and about those who will live in the future.

I think about many different kinds of death.

I'd seen something horribly sad at the amusement park. "The Giant Ferris Wheel" had on a big black ribbon, and it was folding itself up.

The owner of the amusement park must have decided it would cost too much to call in the workers whose job it was to dismantle the rides, and hit on the idea of ordering "The Giant Ferris Wheel" to dispose of itself.

I sat on a swing and watched "The Giant Ferris Wheel" commit suicide.

"The Giant Ferris Wheel" kept rotating its circular frame, yanking off the little carriages where its riders used to sit. It removed one, then another, then another. Every time it pulled off a carriage it bled and cried out in pain. "Oh, it hurts!" it yelled, "It hurts!" Once the circular frame had removed the last carriage, it set about cutting away the circular frames at the center; after that the concrete supports struggled to sever the axle.

Splattered with blood, "The Giant Ferris Wheel" continued to dismantle itself, and at every step along the way it screamed so awfully that the entire amusement park trembled.

"The Merry-Go-Round," which was just next door, sat there shaking with its eyes squeezed shut, covering its ears with its hands.

Finally only the concrete base remained. Its breath came in gasps. Nothing but this block of concrete indicated that "The Giant Ferris Wheel" had ever existed: the block was "The Giant Ferris Wheel"'s ego, its self.

I wondered how the base would finish the job.

There wasn't anything left to do.

"Eat shit and die!"

Leaving these bitter last words, the concrete base put an end to it all.

It did this in a way no human would ever think up.

4.

It keeps growing dark, then growing light again.

There must be a strong wind blowing way up high in the sky.

Song Book is sunk in thought; her head still rests on my shoulder.

Whether she's thinking about the dead, like me, or about the gangsters, or about her old lovers, or about something I can't even imagine, I have no idea.

Song Book is wearing one of my shirts.

It's one of those baggy work shirts. She has nothing on underneath it. That means no bra, of course. It's how I've asked her to dress. I always get the feeling that I'm committing some sort of criminal act when I have to unfasten her bra and take it off, so I've asked her not to wear one.

Having a braless Song Book sitting beside me makes me feel extremely relaxed. I know Song Book's breasts—I know the breasts under that shirt—perfectly. They're not extraordinarily big, but they have a great shape. They're like bowls, and it doesn't matter whether she's leaning backwards or forwards or standing up or what—they hardly change at all.

I know Song Book's whole body perfectly. She doesn't have many split hairs. I figure it's because she's never at all sloppy about taking care of her hair. Separating her hair into several different bunches, she twists each into the shape of a cruller donut, and rubs it up toward the roots. This causes the split ends to pop out, and keeps her hair from growing to different lengths.

The whites of Song Book's eyes are very white.

Sometimes they even turn a little blue, like the eyes of a three-year-old.

I know the moments when her nostrils tend to flare, just a little; and the particular way in which both of her lips are so full; and I know that her clavicle hardly curves at all.

I know the black, soft, smallish patch of her pubic hair, and her genitals.

I know nothing about Song Book's soul. I don't even know my own.

Perhaps there's no such thing as a soul. I can't imagine what purpose souls would serve, even if we did have them. It seems to me that if you're going to kiss someone, it's bound to feel nicer doing it with lips than with a soul.

I gave Song Book a kiss.

5.

Opening one of my eyes just a crack as we kissed, I saw that "Henry IV" had grown weary of thinking and that the vodka had put him in a very mellow mood and that he had curled up into a ball and was now sound asleep.

"Nei-i-i-g-g-h-h," said "Henry IV" in his sleep.

"He's dreaming he's a horse," I said.

"Ble-e-e-e-e-e-eat," said "Henry IV" in his sleep.

"He's dreaming he's a goat," Song Book said.

"Henry IV" said something in his sleep that I was completely unable to decipher. Neither Song Book nor I could make heads or tails of it. Really, neither of us had the faintest idea what it was.

6.

Above the sixth floor is the seventh floor.

They say that on the seventh floor there's a hospital and a junior high and a daycare center. I haven't been up there yet, so I can't be more specific.

They say the hospital isn't at all like a hospital, that the junior high isn't at all like a junior high, and that the daycare center isn't at all like a daycare center.

7.

I'm in "The Poetry School" now, waiting for my students to arrive. "The Poetry School" has only one classroom. Classrooms of "The Poetry School" used to take up the whole B2 floor.

Tens of thousands of people used to study poetry here. Tens of thousands of our school's students once raised their voices in unison, reciting poems by John Berryman and Emily Dickinson. Incredible. It must have been so incredible.

I love John Berryman and Emily Dickinson.

8.

Poetry went out of fashion.

That's why we only have one classroom now.

Why don't I explain to you what the classroom is like.

The classroom is a perfect square in shape, and it is precisely twelve paces long. I just walked the length of the room to measure it.

That's about twice as deep as a standard-issue isolation cell.

That means the area of the classroom is about six times that of a standard-issue isloation cell, and just a bit larger than a cell for more than one prisoner.

The illustrious legal philosopher Gustav Radbruch has considered the problem of the size of isolation cells. Why is it, he asks, that a member of the United States Congress indicted on charges of corruption, a devotee of permanent world revolution convicted of thought crimes, and a youth so madly in love with Judy Garland that he sent Betty Hutton a fan letter with a razor in it when she replaced Garland as the lead in *Annie Get Your Gun* are all confined in cells of the same dimensions? Hey, I'm not making this up. It's right there in Radbruch's collected works.

Radbruch is honest enough to admit that he "doesn't know."

"I must admit that certain aspects of law remain obscure. And the problem of the origin of law must be counted among these."

Five people have discovered the answer to the Area Problem:
Kant
Pashukanis
Dostoyevski
Me
Michel Foucault

Surprisingly, the answer I came up with is exactly the same as the one Foucault hit upon in his book *Discipline and Punish: The Birth of the Prison.*
I didn't cheat on this or anything.
I suppose it's a result of our shared critical consciousness.

The reason isolation cells are all the same size, irrespective of differences in the prisoners' personalities and the nature of their crimes, is that **THE MOMENT YOU START MAKING CELLS OF DIFFERENT SIZES YOU CEASE TO BE ABLE TO DISTINGUISH THE PRISONERS FROM THE GUARDS.**

Kant and Michel Foucault approached the problem theoretically.

Dostoyevski and I approached the problem experimentally.

Pashukanis was lucky: after considering the problem theoretically, he was given a chance to approach it experimentally. When it rains it pours, as they say.

Just before Pashukanis was shot, he sent a list of queries to the Supreme Court.

(1) I would like to be given notification of the date and hour of my execution. Lately the notices have been arriving after the deed has been carried out. I'm telling you, the judicial authorities are getting slack.

(2) What is the official title of the crime of which I've been convicted? And is that crime really found in the criminal code? Don't try to lie to me, now. I wrote about half the criminal code myself, you know.

(3) Another matter that concerns me: I hear that at Piatakov's trial the judge, the prosecutor, and the defendant's lawyer were all one and the same man. Couldn't you at least have had the fellow wear a mask or stick on a pair of false whiskers or something? Show a little respect for the fundamental procedures of the law.

(4) I have just received a copy of the indictment. But the date I'm supposed to have commenced my secret communications with the counterrevolutionaries postdates that of the beginning of my incarceration here. Is this prison managed by the White Army? Don't come whining to me if you all end up getting jugged yourselves, right on up to the Minister of Justice.

(5) It pains me to have to say this, but the prosecutor in charge of my case was completely incompetent. With a jackass like him running the show, some-

one who really deserves to be found guilty would end up getting off. So, how would you guys feel about creating a special provision in my case and allow me to serve as the prosecutor in charge of prosecuting myself? I'm confident I can bring home a guilty verdict.

According to Pashukanis, the fact that all isolation cells are the same size is **PURELY A MATTER OF THE COST OF CONSTRUCTING THEM.**

The day of the execution came.

The soldier from the Red Army who tied the blindfold over Pashukanis's eyes asked Pashukanis a question as he tied the blindfold.

"How about it doc, one last 'Three Cheers for Stalin'?"

"Are you an idiot?" replied Pashukanis.

Pashukanis kept his head turned to the side as the shot was fired, so the bullet penetrated his temple.

That's how big the classroom is. I hope I've made myself clear.

9.

A blackboard hangs in the classroom. As a matter of fact we've even got chalk. White, red, yellow, blue, green, pink, and Prussian-blue chalk.

When I write Rimbaud's "Dawn" on the blackboard, I use cream-yellow chalk.

For Housman's "Song of the Wind," I use green-grass green chalk.

I use coffee-colored chalk for Trakl's whole oeuvre. That's Song Book's idea.

The poems don't seem very Trakl-esque when you write them in yellow chalk. His poems aren't obtrusive; they just seem to drift down.

Rilke's are the only poems I know that never seem to work in any color. His poems aren't the kind of things you can write on a blackboard.

10.

There are also chairs and desks. Small chairs and desks, made of wood.

They're arranged like this:

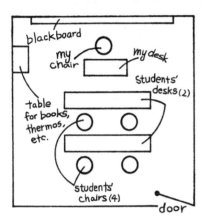

There are no windows.

Right, drawing everything out like this has reminded me that there's a table where I can put my thermos and books and stuff.

11.

I've got a thermos full of hot coffee on the table. Usually I bring books as well, but today I don't have any books.

Just the thermos.

The thermos is full of "Song Book's Blend."

"Song Book's Blend" is made by mixing equal amounts of Mocha and Mandarin and then adding a smidgen of Costa Rica. Song Book prepares it all.

I drink coffee while I wait for the students to arrive.

12.

I was forgetting something very important.
A vampire lives in the room next to the classroom.

13.

Only he's very quiet.

When you put your ear up against the blackboard, you can just barely make out the voice of the vampire singing on the other side of the concrete wall.

The vampire's voice is so soft that I can't even tell what he's singing.

No one has ever seen the vampire, and we're not even sure how to get into the next room. All the rooms on the second basement floor except for the classroom I'm sitting in now have been sealed off with concrete.

The vampire seems very subdued and introspective.

The vampire clumps slowly across the floor, and sits in his squeaky chair.

The vampire goes to the bathroom, just like the rest of us.

If nothing else, you can hear the sound of the vampire's toilet when he flushes. You don't even have to put your ear to the blackboard.

Even after the noise of the rushing water stops, the pipes of the vampire's toilet keep gurgling for an extremely long time: "Glumpglomp glumpglomp."

There's something wrong with the sewage pipes.

"Glumpglomp glumpglomp glumpglomp glumpglomp glumpglomp."

If the pipes of the vampire's toilet start gurgling during class, the students and I sit there listening, concentrating intently on the sound.

Right now I'm putting my ear to the blackboard, wondering what on earth that song could be that the vampire is always singing.

To my ears, it kind of sounds like this:

"Who's afraid of vampires?"

14.

My teaching here isn't focused on knowledge.

If you want to know about poetry, read books. You'll find all that in books.

My knowledge of poetry is both fragmented and fuzzy. It can't be trusted.

I don't teach people how to interpret poetry or any of that stuff either.

I'm not so good at interpreting poetry.

When I read a poem, I respond to it in one of two ways: "Wow, this is great!" or "God, this is awful!" I have no other responses.

Having eliminated those possibilities, we are left with "How to create poetry." Surely that must be what the man teaches! That's what you're all thinking, right? Hell, that's what I'm thinking myself.

But the truth is that if there really were some technique that permitted everybody who knew it to write wonderful poems, I'd want to be the first to know.

If I had a technique like that, I'd keep it all to myself and produce one masterpiece after another, setting my sights on the Nobel Prize for Poets.

I'm a poet, but even now I have no idea how I write my poems.

I really doubt there is a technique to writing poetry.

We poets spend the eyeblink of time granted us until we slip away forever into the eternal dark composing poems, never having the faintest idea how we ought to go about writing them, or what we ought to be writing.

I do almost nothing at all here.

Pressed to explain, I might say that my job is *conducting traffic*.

The students who come here all want to write poems. But none of them have any idea what kind of poems they should be writing.

You mustn't tell them to "Write what you like."

I may be incompetent as a poet, but I don't shirk my responsibilities.

I talk with my students. Or, to make it sound hard, I counsel them.

Actually, for the most part all I do is listen.

Writing poetry is a fairly morbid thing to do. Of course, that doesn't mean all morbid people are poets. It is here, you see, that the difficulty lies.

If any of you out there really and truly and from the very bottom of your heart wants to write poetry, and if on top of that you are troubled by the fact that you don't know how or what to write, I really hope you will enroll in our school.

I will listen to what you have to say.

You will be the one to talk.

I want you to feel free to come and talk about anything you want to talk about, no matter how elusive or embarrassing or unbelievably dull it may be. It will be just the two of us in this basement room, and even if you start talking about sex, rest assured that I won't jump on top of you or anything.

Talking about it is bound to help you relax.

Perhaps you'll tell me that you miscalculated and got it on with your boyfriend on a dangerous day, so you're feeling kind of worried, and as you talk tears will well up in your eyes. And that's okay, if you feel like crying, just go ahead and cry. Hey, you won't be able to cry when you're dead.

In this fashion, all on your own, you'll discover what you should write.

"I'm happy for you, I really am," I'll say, shaking your hand.

Maybe you'll want to start writing poems right away, here in the classroom.

But—hold on.

Wait until you've left this place, until you're by yourself, to start writing.

That's what I'll say to you.

The lighting in here is too dim to write poetry by, and the air is bad.

You'll go out.

And then, in some other, brighter place, you'll begin to write.

I hope that you'll forget me then.

I didn't do anything. You started it all by yourself.

I love this job.

II "Welcome home"

1.

A birdcage stood between the old lady and me.

The theme the old lady wanted to write on lay motionless in the birdcage.

"What's it called, this thing here?" I asked.

"GILA MONSTER," the old lady replied. These were the first words the old lady had spoken since she arrived at "The Poetry School." She seemed to want very badly to say something else. She looked as if she wanted to tell me that she had once been young herself, many years ago, but she was afraid I might call her a liar, and so she couldn't bring herself to speak up.

I just stared and stared at the "GILA MONSTER," not saying a word. In the entire universe nothing existed but the lady and me and this "GILA MONSTER" between us, and staring at the "GILA MONSTER" was the only sort of entertainment there had ever been since the universe came into being.

"Oh!" cried the old lady. "It moved! The 'GILA MONSTER' moved, didn't it?"

She was right: the "GILA MONSTER" had just advanced about two millimeters or thereabouts across the bottom of the birdcage. Its arms and its legs and its tail hadn't moved a bit, though, and its eyes remained closed.

Once again the "GILA MONSTER" was utterly still.

The old woman and I stared at the birdcage.

"Hey, assholes, cut the crap!" shouted Our Lord at the old

lady and me from the patch of grass where he was reclining, out in the outfield. Our Lord was greatly pissed off. "Man, this universe sure is boring. It's the crappiest universe I ever made. I mean, nothing ever happens here, does it?"

Then the old woman began talking.

"All my life I've lived with this 'GILA MONSTER.' My father used to say that the 'GILA MONSTER' appeared in our house on the day I was born.

I took the 'GILA MONSTER' with me when I got married, too.

My first husband played the trumpet, and whenever he was at home he would sit the 'GILA MONSTER' on his lap and play ballads for us.

My husband died in the war. It was such a sad way to go. The bullet went right through his cheeks. Even after they stitched them up, he was tormented by nightmares and he would bellow in his sleep. 'Ahhh,' he would groan, 'what will I do if smoke leaks from my cheeks?'

The day they removed the stitches, my husband called me to his side.

'I'm going to smoke a cigarette now,' he said. 'Watch closely.'

With trembling hands my husband lit his cigarette, then sucked in a lungful of smoke and slowly exhaled.

'How's it look? No smoke leaking from my cheeks, is there?'

I'll never forget that scene, not even on the other side of Saint Peter's gate.

There was no smoke leaking from my husband's cheeks.

Instead—woe is me!—a line of smoke rose from his right ear.

The smoke drifted up in a perfectly straight line from my husband's right ear, like the fumes belched on a windless day from a trash incinerator smokestack.

My husband just couldn't take the shock.

'I won't be able to play "Round About Midnight" or "Someday My Prince Will Come" if I've got air leaking from the hole in my ear,' murmured my husband, his voice terribly sad, as he lay on his deathbed, holding my hand in his.

Even then, my husband tried to give me strength as I wept and wailed. 'Just think, up in heaven I'll be able to jam with Charlie Parker and Eric Dolphy and all the rest of the gang,' he quipped. 'Let me tell you, when our band plays "Take the A Train," even the Lord Himself will start swinging.'

I was sitting beside my husband's bed.

'Tell me,' said my husband. 'What exactly does our "GILA MONSTER" look like? I'm having trouble calling it to mind.'

I gazed into the birdcage at the 'GILA MONSTER' and tried to come up with some way to describe it to my husband. But I wasn't able to do it. *No matter how long or how hard I think, I can't find the right words to describe the* 'GILA MONSTER.'

'I'm afraid I can't quite describe it,' I told my husband.

'Oh well, too bad.'

These were my husband's last words.

I remarried. Naturally I took the 'GILA MONSTER' with

me.

My new husband wouldn't tell me what his job was.

'It's an extremely nerve-racking, delicate job that helps a lot of people,' was all he would say, and he was always saying it. He was also a man of intense faith, and so, whenever we performed our marital duties, he would require that I get down on all fours, and he was quite averse to touching his own *thing* himself.

In all other respects, I found him an extremely gentle, good person. And of course he showered affection on my 'GILA MONSTER' as well.

My second husband also had the misfortune to meet with a dreadful accident at his place of work. His face was completely burned off.

Somehow or other his head caught fire. They told me he sprinted a full 100 meters when it happened, howling an absolutely terrible howl, his face enveloped in flames. The colleague who brought him home told me about it. 'It was as if the Olympic torch had leapt from its post and joined the 100 meter dash,' he said.

My husband breathed his last only three hours or so after he arrived home.

My husband kept stroking his bandaged face, telling me again and again how sad it made him feel not to have a face anymore.

When I touched my husband's face with my hands, there were no traces left of the old bumps or hollows—even he was unable to say precisely where his eyes or nose or mouth were.

I cut a piece of cardboard into the shape of a face and made holes where the eyes and mouth were supposed to be; then for the nose I used Cemedine to stick on a few little bits left over from the cutting. As soon as I had finished, I lay the cardboard cutout down on top of my husband's face.

'It's a face, darling. It's your face.'

I lifted my husband's hands to his cardboard face.

'Oh wow, I've got a *face*. No mistaking it, it's my face! It's very handsome.'

Clasping his cardboard face in his arms, my husband finally grew calm.

'Tell me,' said my husband. I had the impression that now that the problem of his face had been dealt with, he had been letting his mind wander, trying to see if there weren't any other matters he needed to take care of before he died. 'What exactly does our "GILA MONSTER" look like? I'm having trouble calling it to mind.'

I couldn't describe it this time either. I simply can't come up with the right words to describe what the 'GILA MONSTER' looks like.

'I'm afraid I can't quite describe it.'

'Oh well, too bad.'

Of course my husband died after that."

The old lady seemed very youthful when she talked about her dead husbands. In the sense that someone who's actually 120 might look as if she's only 85 or so.

"Just look at me, how dreadfully old I've gotten. I try to live my days so that I'm always ready, so it won't matter when He comes to get me," said the old lady. "But there's still one thing that troubles me."

The old lady smiled at the "GILA MONSTER" in the bird-cage.

The "GILA MONSTER" was still suction-cupped to the bottom of the cage, lying so still that it seemed to have nothing whatsoever to do with our universe.

"I want to try capturing in words what this 'GILA MONSTER' looks like. And then I want to take the paper on which I've written those words and go join my husbands in the place where they've gone."

"Have you ever actually tried to write about this . . . 'GILA MONSTER'?"

"Yes . . . but no matter how many times I try, I'm unable to do it."

I observed the motionless "GILA MONSTER."

Then I wrote the following words on the blackboard.

—O "GILA MONSTER"!
You have green, slimy skin
You have webs between each of the five fingers on your
        hands
And folded eyelids
Long, thick hind legs   a tail just as thick
and perfectly straight
O "GILA MONSTER"!—

I put down the chalk and looked over at the cage.

The "GILA MONSTER" was lying there just as still as ever. Except that now it had brown skin covered all over with bumps, and its two hands had grown hooves, which were cloven, and there was a horn between its eyes, and it had no tail at all.

"This is what always happens," said the old lady with a sad smile.

Once more I took up the chalk.

—O brown-skinned, bump-covered "GILA MONSTER"!
How the hell did you manage to give yourself cloven
       hooves
And grow a horn between your eyes
And how did you get rid of your tail?—

Evidently the "GILA MONSTER" wasn't very pleased with the poem I had written, because it began vigorously flapping its gigantic wings and glared suspiciously at me with three of its four eyes while adroitly scratching its back with its two tails.

I sat down in my chair.

Between us, the "GILA MONSTER" resumed its posture.

Staggered, Our Lord betook himself to some other ballpark.

"Do you think it's impossible?" asked the old lady.

Is poetry without any power at all?

I whispered something into the old lady's ear.

The old lady stood up, went to the blackboard, and took up a piece of chalk.

I remained silent.

The old lady was thinking.

The "GILA MONSTER" remained still.

The old lady wrote on the blackboard in characters very neat and easy to read, taking her time. When she finished writing, she turned to look at the birdcage. The "GILA MON-

STER" had become what was written on the blackboard.

"Oh, it's wonderful!"

Setting down the chalk, the old lady gave me a kiss on the forehead. She was so excited that her lips had grown warm.

After the old lady left, I sat gazing at the poem she had left on the board.

I bet you're all kind of interested to know what sort of poem the old lady wrote. But there's no way for me to communicate it to you.

I can't translate it into words you would understand.

Neither could anyone else.

2.

Dana Do Bumbum
Chuchu-Elia IX d'Oricas
Alan Twilight
Floribellechel Flor
Nordiska Sonata

The boys (or girls?) were quintuplets, and they resembled each other so closely that I doubted even their own parents could tell them apart.

Since there are only four chairs here, the boys (or girls?) catapulted themselves into a game of musical chairs the instant they entered the classroom, manifesting a fighting spirit so savage it was frightening.

The lone loser came rocketing out from the middle of the war that was taking place among the five kids with their identical faces, shorts, and T-shirts, and the fighting ground to a halt.

I turned to the boy (or girl?) sitting on the left in the front row.

He/she was picking his/her nose.

"Dana Do Bumbum, what does your mother want you to learn here?"

"You've got the wrong dude, man. I'm Chuchu-Elia IX d'Oricas."

I turned to the boy (or girl?) sitting on the right in the front row.

He/she was admiring the snot he/she had picked from

his/her nose.

"Dana Do Bumbum, what does your mother want you to learn here?"

"You've got the wrong dude. I'm Alan Twilight."

I turned to the boy (or girl?) sitting on the left in the back row.

He/she was whacking the kid on the left in the front row over his/her head.

"Dana Do Bumbum, what did your mother . . ."

"You've got the wrong dude, damn it! I'm Floribellechel Flor!"

I turned to the boy (or girl?) sitting on the right in the back row.

He/she had just been spit upon by the kid on the right in the front row, and was working rapidly to store up munitions to fire back in return.

"Dana Do Bumbum."

"Listen, you jerk, I'm Nordiska Sonata! Aww, man, what a pisshead you are! I went to all the trouble of gathering that spit, and you made me swallow it!"

I turned to the boy (or girl?) who had been left standing.

He/she was weeping quietly.

"Dana Do Bumbum, what did your mother tell you to learn here?"

The boy (or girl?) continued to weep quietly as he/she replied:

"Dana Do Bumbum is a sneak! The damn bully shoved me out of my chair while you were talking. I'm Chuchu-

Elia IX d'Oricas."

As if this had been the signal, the chair-stealing war broke out anew.

If I don't get another chair, I'll never learn their names.

3.

Sitting before me was a girl who looked like she must be in eighth grade or so. She wore a school uniform. Her hair was in braids, and she had a broad forehead.

"It's so tragic when a girl in eighth grade is plain," said the girl.

"Take a look in the mirror. You just don't have any meat on you yet, that's all. I think you'll be a really pretty girl in another year or so," I countered.

There was a telephone on my desk. The girl had brought it with her.

This telephone was the problem.

"When did you start getting these calls?"

"About six months ago. In the beginning I thought it was someone with the wrong number, you know? My friends kept insisting that it was a prank caller, that's what they said. The calls never come when my mom and dad are around. And then when I told my mom about it, she told me that I was either reading too many books or studying too hard. Can you believe it? She drives me crazy!"

"Have you been to see a doctor?"

"Yeah. And guess what this dumbass doctor says to my mom. He tells her, 'It's an illusion fostered by your daughter's sexual desires. Cases like this are not at all uncommon among pubescent youths, and my advice to you is to attempt, little by little, to relieve her of some of this frustration.' Man, these doctors drive me wild, they really do! So now everyone at home, my mom and my dad and my grandpa and my grandma, every one of them, they spend the whole day just sitting around reading Freud and Jung and Adler, and then they observe me. It's hell, it really is. I get up in the morning, right, and my mom is sitting there by my bed, and she asks me, 'Did you sleep well, honey? What kind of dreams did you have?' I go and sit down at the table for breakfast and my dad says, 'What comes to mind when you think of the words "ham" and "eggs"?'

So I run off, feeling relieved to escape it all, and I go out to the veranda where grandpa's taking it easy in a patch of sun, and he points at these splotches on the sheets hanging out next door, where the neighbors' baby took a leak in its sleep, and he says, 'Tell me, what does that look like to you?'

It's simply unbearable."

"Yeah, that sounds pretty awful."

The girl gets these telephone calls. They're from some guy she doesn't know. Speaking in an extremely serious, earnest tone, the guy explains that he doesn't know where he is, and says he'd be grateful if she could tell him.

But the girl isn't able to help.

She has no idea where he is.

"I wish I could tell him, but I just don't know."

The girl's eyes filled with tears. A nice girl.

She didn't know what to do anymore, so she came here. Giving advice to girls like this is part of my job.

The girl and I waited for the telephone to ring.

"I'm really sorry I came to you with such a strange problem. I mean, it's not at all poetic or anything, is it?"

"Oh, I wouldn't say that."

The telephone rang.

The girl picked up the receiver.

"Hello! Listen, today, I may be able to tell you where you are . . . Yeah, listen, I've got someone here who knows about that sort of thing, I'm going to pass you over to him now, okay, so don't hang up."

I took the receiver from the girl.

"C'mon, c'mon! Just tell me where I am!"

The man was shouting right from the start.

"All right now, just calm down. Tell me what happened."

"I turned down the wrong street! I don't know where I am!! Help me!"

"Roger. I understand. Now, tell me what you see around you."

The man fell silent for a second. He was clearly looking around.

"Uhhh . . . hmm, there's a big store with a glass front in the direction I'm facing. There's a sign."

"Read me the letters on the sign."

"T. I. F. Another F. A. N. Y. That's it."

"T, I, F, F, A, N, Y? Is that right? Well then, it sounds like you must be in New York. Is there a tall building over to the left?"

"No, no, I don't see anything like that . . . over to the left there's this enormous mountain, the peak is covered with snow, and then . . . oh wow, there's this huge herd of giraffes down by the foothills."

"Okay, then maybe it's the Natural Preserve in Kenya. What do you see over to the right? Can you see any grasslands?"

"Nope. Golly, what a surprise *this* is. There's a *wall*. I'd say it must be about one hundred . . . no, maybe two hundred yards tall. Appears to be made of bricks. There's no entrance or exit of any sort or anything."

"And behind the wall? What's behind the wall?"

"Behind it? Oh, right, I see, I see, you mean behind it! Let's see, there's . . . Oh my goodness. O-h-h-h MY goodness! Oh my GOODNESS."

The man began guffawing into the phone.

"Whoo-ee, that's really something. Sorry to start laughing like that. See if you can guess what I'm seeing behind the wall. Man, that's really something."

"What do you see?"

"President Kennedy is giving a speech! What's more, he's got Mitch Miller and the Gang standing in a cluster around him. Every time President Kennedy tries to speak, Mitch Miller and the Gang sings along with him in chorus.

Yow! It's no good, I must have lost my mind!"

"All right, I want you to calm down. Just keep calm and listen to what I have to say, all right? You haven't lost your mind. You're in the first track on the A side of *Sing Along With JFK*. The song is called 'Let Us Begin Beguine.' Have you got that? Are you listening to me?

You're in a record. Do you understand? Hello?!"

There was no answer.

The man was sobbing.

"Hello?!!" I shouted.

"Where am I? It's weird here, I don't wanna be here anymore. I don't like it here." The man was talking to himself, his voice choked with tears. He couldn't hear what I was saying. "Oh God, where the hell am I?!!"

The line went dead.

I sat without moving, the receiver in my hand.

"What happened?" the girl asked, looking concerned. "Did it seem like he'd figured out where he is?"

What was I supposed to tell her?

How could I explain things in a way an eighth grade girl surrounded by psychoanalyst moms, dads, and grandpas would understand?

"It's unfortunate, but he didn't seem able to figure it out. I told him how to go about discovering where he is, though, so I think if he can just calm down a little he'll manage to put it all together.

He's an adult, after all. Don't worry, I don't think you'll be getting any more calls from him," I said.

The girl smiled happily. She would be much prettier in another year.

"Muchibus thankibus, Mr. Teacher."

The girl stuffed the telephone into her huge shoulder bag and stood up.

"Mr. Teacher, can I ask you a question?"

"Sure."

"It's about this."

The girl pointed to the Snoopy printed on her bag.

On the bag, Snoopy was lying on the roof of his doghouse, taking a nap.

"Why is there a Van Gogh painting hanging in his doghouse?" asked the girl.

"Sorry, but I really have no idea," I replied.

Having lobbed me this mysterious query, the girl went back aboveground.

I figure the girl will write a poem when she turns sixteen or seventeen. And there's no doubt in my mind that her poem will be about "the telephone," and that the person on the other end of the line will be a young man who doesn't give a fig whether he knows what he is or not.

Be that as it may, Charlie Brown!
Why is it that Snoopy likes *The Night Cafe*?

4.

I have no idea how much it costs to attend a class at "The Poetry School." Or how the students make the payments. Sometimes all I get is an ice cream.

There was nothing I could do about that in the case of this boy. Because the work I did for him wasn't worth any more than an ice cream.

The boy dropped a heavy stack of books on his desk. He had the *Astronomical Almanac, A Comprehensive Table of Fixed Stars, Photographs of the Stars Taken Using Mount Palomar Observatory's 200-inch Hale Telescope*, Ursula Kroeber Le Guin's "Lions of Mars," a stack of Sunspot Observation Forms, and Romain Rolland's *The Leonid Meteors*. He had bought the last of these by mistake.

"I want to write a poem."

"About stargazing, right?"

The boy goggled. My guess had hit the mark.

"Wow, Mr. Teacher, you've got telepathy!"

"Of course."

I was happy that my guess had proved correct.

"Do you want an ice cream?" the boy asked.

"Sure."

The boy had bought two ice creams on the way, one for him and one for me. One vanilla, one chocolate. I opted for the chocolate.

"The problem is that I don't know how to write it," said the boy, taking a lick of his vanilla ice cream.

"Write it however you want," I replied, taking a lick of my chocolate ice cream.

"But there are all sorts of issues one needs to address, right? Is it better to use the colloquial or the traditional literary style, for example, and should I write my piece in prose or in verse, should I make it a sonnet, is it best not to use too many similes, is it true that 'My inner "King of the Moment" is dead,' as the poet Tanigawa Gan said? Don't I need to consider these things?" asked vanilla-boy.

Uh oh. This is not good, not good at all. Vanilla-boy has been reading those scary writings they call *poetry criticism.* Doesn't he know you're not supposed to read that stuff until you're older?

"Okay, listen up," I said. " 'Anything you think is a poem is a poem. Even if others think something is a poem, it's not a poem unless you think it's a poem.' Do you know who taught me that?"

"Nope."

"The Martians. They took me to the mother ship, and I learned it there."

Vanilla-boy was so thrilled he leapt from his seat.

It was the first time he'd met someone who'd actually had a close encounter of the third kind.

Vanilla-boy was kind enough to show me the records he kept of his stargazing. Vanilla-boy had been stargazing ever since he was three.

"These are all poems," I said.

Vanilla-boy went home extremely pleased. And why not? The lucky devil had just learned he'd been writing poems every day since he was three.

Vanilla-boy's stargazing records went like this:

Observations of the Milky Way carried out with an opera glass:

(1) The average speed of the Milky Way, measured over a period of one year, is 3 knots per hour.

(2) During June and September, there are many days when the speed climbs up past 5 knots. I suspect this is due to the rain.

(3) During February, on the other hand, the speed is greatly reduced. On some days the Milky Way appears to have come to a total stop when observed through an opera glass. This is because the outer surface freezes. Still, if I look at it after attaching my orthoscopic 5 mm eyepiece to my 15 cm reflector, I can see that the stars are flowing by at a very languid pace beneath the icy surface.

(4) According to the *Science Almanac*, the average speed of the Milky Way over the period of a year around the year 1500 on the Western calendar was 5 knots.

5.

"Virgil's the name, but all my pals call me Maro," said "The Refrigerator."

A General Motors 3 door commercial refrigerator/freezer sat before me.

I listened to it talk, feeling extremely nervous.

This was the first time I had ever spoken to Virgil, the great father of all poets, and it was also the first time I had ever spoken to a refrigerator.

"No need to play the stuffed parrot with me, my friend," said the refrigerator. "You're the teacher here, after all. I'm just the student. Catch my drift?"

"I'm sorry, Virgil, but I just don't think that's going to work. There isn't a poet alive who wouldn't feel honored to meet you."

"Don't be an ass. I'm no longer an acting poet, I'm just one of the Old Boys. And let's face it, being an Old Boy doesn't count for anything in poetry. You'd agree with me there, right? Come on, I'm not even a person anymore. Just look at me, I'm a refrigerator."

In order to relieve my tension, I cracked a few knuckles.

Cr-a-a-ck. Cr-a-a-ck. Cr-a-a-a-a-ck. Cr-a-a-a-a-a-a-ck.

"I had a hell of a time getting here, a hell of a time," said Virgil the Fridge.

When he tried to get on the train the conductor barricaded his way, telling him that electric appliances were prohibited from riding, and the doors of the taxis were so small that he couldn't squeeze through, and when he gave up and decided to walk, some dimwitted rapscallion had tried to make off with him.

"Goodness. What did you do?"

"I shouted at him. 'Impudent wretch!' I cried, 'Darest thou lay a finger on the great Virgil!!!' As soon as he heard that, the little ninny ran off shrieking."

The first act of this tragedy took place at a party at Virgil's house.

"I had a reunion at my place. Quite a few of the old guys were good enough to drop by—Hesiod was there, and Alcaeus, and Anacreon, and Pindar—and everyone seemed to be having a grand old time. Of course there were also a few like Empedocles who had gone totally senile, but that was no big deal.

'Hey, Empedocles! Long time no see!'

'Ah, quite. And, ah, who might you be?'

'I'm Virgil, old chum, Virgil.'

'Ah, quite. And, ah, who might you be?'

'I'm Virgil, old chum, Virgil.'

'Ah, quite. And, ah, who might you be?'

Such a pitiful sight, old Empedocles!

But Ovid was worst of all.

It gave us all quite a shock to see how cruelly time had altered him. He was pickled to the gills when he showed up, and believe me, whoo-o-o-e-ee, the stench he gave off was like nothing in this world! Seemed the man possessed not a shred of clothing but the scrap he wore on his back, which was filthy as filthy could be, let me tell you! and which, now that we were looking more closely, had a certain something about it that seemed to suggest it might be doubling or rather tripling as both his bed and bedroom.

'Hi there! Hup hup! Damn it, varlet! More wine!'

'Haven't you had enough, man? Wait until you've sober-ed up a bit.'

'Skinflint! Stingy bastard! You realize this is Ovid you're talking to? Ovid!! Don't you play high and mighty with ME, damn you! Bring more wine! Dear God, may every one of these scoundrels burn in hell!'

'Cool it, will you? We came here to have fun, not to hear you rant.'

'Yeah, big deal, bub. A bunch of half-assed poets and two-bit porno novelists getting together to have themselves a little fling! Whoopteedoo! Damned little pissheads! Hey! Hey Aeschylus! Why the hell are you looking at me like that, huh? Huh? You got something you want to say to me? You know I saw that fucking drama of yours, bud. I've only so much time in this life of mine, and boy was that thing a waste. You wanna waste my precious time, huh, that what you want? I want that time back, you hear! Dirty thief!

Where's Aristophanes? Your comedies *suck*, you hear that? S-U-C-K spells SUCK, and man do your comedies SUCK. Given the choice between watching one of your foul comedies and watching a tour guide flail around after falling into a barrel of night soil, I'd much prefer to watch the latter. Because that would be a hell of a lot funnier, bub, let me tell you.'

'That's enough, Ovid. If you keep mouthing off like this

you'll have to go.'

As soon as I'd said this, huge tears started streaming down Ovid's cheeks.

'Oh, how cruel! How terribly cruel! Who would have thought that Maro of all people would ever say such a thing! My whole life is in shambles, everything falling to pieces around me . . . how can you be so heartless as to treat me like this! Sniffle sniffle. I guess it's not enough for you just to chase me out of Rome and take all the wealth and honor and glory for yourself, huh? What do you say to that, huh? Why should I, the author of *Metamorphoses*, be the only one to live my life in abject poverty, shivering from the cold? Why?'

Ovid, my dear old friend, was suffering from alcoholism, paranoid delusions, and malnutrition. I gave the poor wreck a hug.

'Listen to me, Naso. And I want you to pay close attention, okay? No one hates you. You have no idea how terribly sad we all were when you were chased out of Rome like that. We presented a petition to the Senate, and we even went to discuss your case with Augustus himself. The copyright for *Metamorphoses* has expired, but the PEN Club is holding your royalties for you. And while nowadays no one but a few whimsical dabblers has any interest in any of the works the rest of us wrote, your *Metamorphoses* is still in active service, shooting its guns off like nobody's business. For Pete's sake, the thing has been translated into over one hundred and thirty languages around the world, and everyone from preschoolers to the chief of the Navaho

tribe is reading it. All the poets and novelists in the world are virtually your grandchildren. That's the truth, old boy.
Hey, everyone, isn't that so?'
'Absolutely! You bet!' agreed Aeschylus and Hesiod and Aristophanes.
Ovid continued to sob.
'I'm sorry, guys, I'm so sorry, really, I'm so sorry I said all those awful things. I just felt that I'd been left behind, you know, I just felt so lonely.'
'It's okay, Naso, don't cry! Nobody is angry with you. Here, wipe your tears with this hanky, there you go, just have a seat in this chair here. You probably want something to drink? Now, let me bring something over for you. What'll it be, you want a bourbon on the rocks, just like old times?'
'Thanks, Maro. My doctor says I can't have bourbon. I mean, I don't really let that bother me much most of the time . . . but perhaps I'll have a manhattan. Go light on the whisky and heavy on the vermouth, if you will.'
'Sure thing, old chum,' I said, giving Ovid a wink. 'One manhattan, light on whisky and heavy on vermouth. Coming right up.'
Dante and Beatrice were perched on a sofa way over in the corner of the room, drinking egg wine. Dante had a sort of jolly-old-geezer look about him that made you think his grandchildren must be really adorable, and Beatrice had turned into an extremely elegant old lady. The two of them were holding hands, looking as if they had made up their minds never to part again, not even for a moment.
'Ah, Beatrice my dear, you're still as lovely as ever.'

'Flattery that transparent won't get you anywhere, Maro.'

'That's right, Maro. Enough of that, it'll only go to her head.'

We talked of our memories. Looking back on it now, that tortuous 'descent into hell' seemed like a sweet and beautiful adventure.

'You were so manly then, darling. How wonderful you were.'

'No, Beatrice my dear, you were the wonderful one.'

The aged couple sat on the sofa gazing into each other's eyes, tightly clasping each other's hands. It seemed tactful to slip away and leave them alone.

Back in the middle of the room, Hesiod was just giving Ovid a good scolding, trying to tear him away from Empedocles.

'Damn you, you doddering old wretch, why aren't you dead? I thought you'd thrown yourself into Mt. Etna or something. What the hell's up with you?'

'Ah, quite. And, ah, who might you be?'

'You making fun of me? Right, I'll fix you! Step outside, buddy!'

'Stop it, Naso, just stop it. Empedocles is getting old, too, you know.'

'Piss off, asshole! Hey there, Empedocles! How'd you like for me to take you back to Mt. Etna again, take a little trip, huh? How's that sound to you?'

'Ah, quite. And, ah, who might you be?'

'Okay, okay. I'll tell you my name, you moron. Here be-

fore you stands the great Ovid himself! Ovid! And now,
worm, I'll recite a line from my masterpiece.
Aequatae spirant aurae, datur hora quieti.
(Ah, so you're to die. It's been a long day.)
Got that, gramps?'
Empedocles spat a great gob of phlegm onto the floor,
shoved his hands down into his pockets, and burst into
speech. 'What on earth are you talking about, kid? That was
the last phrase of the fifth book of *The Aeneid*. It's a line of
Virgil's, not yours. You'd better be a little more careful if
you want to start plagiarizing. As far as I know, there isn't
a single phrase of that exalted caliber in your entire oeuvre.
To tell the truth, I think you'd be wise to edit your own stuff
some if you've got so much free time on your hands that
you can piddle around getting pie-eyed and shooting your
damn mouth off. Why not give that a thought, kid, eh? Do
you a world of good, if you ask me.'

As soon as he'd finished speaking, Empedocles let his
shoulders droop back down and once more started playing
The Senile Old Fool.

'Ah, quite. And, ah, who might you be?'

'Let me at him!! Hesiod! I beg you, let me go!! I'll kill
the bastard, I will!! I swear I'm gonna wring that old fart's
neck!!'

When the reunion was over, everyone left but Ovid,
who was dead drunk.

'Naso, there's a bed you can sleep in.'

'Beds, beds—who needs 'em. I can only get to sleep when
I'm under a couch. Tell me, sir, what's poetic about a bed,

huh? I myself am of the opinion, you see, that the bed is for the heavy-lidded poet a most ill-suited item of furniture.

Pontum adspectabant flentes

(Tears sprang to my eyes as I gazed upon the sea)

Ah yes, how romantic. How about that, Maro—is that one I wrote myself or is it one of yours?'

'I think it's yours, Naso.'

'Really? I come up with some good stuff, huh? Yeah, not bad, not bad. . . .'

I put a blanket over Ovid, who lay there with his arms wrapped around the leg of the sofa, having muttered himself to sleep, then brought over a washbasin and positioned it nearby. After that I went off to my bedroom.

Rocking in a storm of tangled emotions, I fell asleep. I had no dreams.

And when I woke the next morning, I'd turned into a refrigerator," said Virgil.

"I'll bet that must have been quite a shock."

"Yes, it was a shock all right. At first I thought I was just having an unpleasant dream, something brought on by the alcohol. So I kept waiting to wake up, you know, but there was no sign that it was ever going to happen. So I began to think it wasn't a dream, after all. It occurred to me that perhaps I had lost my mind, so I decided to test myself by trying to recite a poem I'm fond of.

'Turn the corner

Once more   turn the corner

Once again   turn the corner
You turn the corner
Once more   you turn the corner
Once again   you turn the corner
Don't get annoyed!
They're corners.'

I recited it perfectly. *So it was true. I'd metamorphosed into a refrigerator!*

I peered around to see whether or not there was a cord coming out of my body. I'd hate to find myself dropping dead all of a sudden just because I'd pulled my plug from the outlet. But there was no cord. *Oh, that's swell,* I thought, *I'm some kind of new model with an internal battery.* Getting up from my bed, I headed to the living room to discuss this new turn of events with Ovid, who was snoring away under the sofa. After all, there's no better person to answer any questions one may have on the subject of metamorphoses.

'Arise, Ovid
From your eternal slumbers!
Arise, ye starvlings
Away with the chains of ignorance that bind our feet
Come, comrades, let us rally!
Wake from your dream of the Satyr's feast
Apollo's light is near.'

'Shut your trap, will you! It doesn't even rhyme, and the wretched thing isn't a sonnet or anything, is it? Repeating

"Arise" like that instead of using alliteration is a cheap trick, nothing but a trick, I'm telling you! Hey! Maro! Give me some water! Water, I say! Water! Oh god, does my head ache!!'

Ovid slowly clambered out from under the sofa and collided with my door.

'Urgh! Damn, that hu-*u-urt*! Hm? Well, well, well. That's service for you. Maro, old boy, you're a pal. A thousand arigatos.'

Ovid grabbed my handle, yanked open my door, and peered inside.

'Maro! Hey, Maro! There's nothing in here, old friend! Do us a favor and get a grip on yourself, huh? The whole idea behind having a refrigerator is that you can put beer and grapefruits and stuff in it when you want to cool them! You don't just have a thing like this sitting around for decoration, you know!'

'Thanks a lot, Naso, I'll try to be more careful from now on. I'm afraid this is the first time I've ever become a refrigerator, you know, so I haven't quite got the hang of it.'

Standing there just as he was, his back straight as a board, Ovid raised both his hands and gave his starboard and portside cheeks a round-trip slap.

'Sweet God above!!!! Catastrophe has struck!!!!

The sickness has finally reached my brain!!!

My liver's bombed out, my pancreas is kaput, my stomach is a mess, my teeth are all rickety, I can't read a newspaper without putting on my glasses, my pecker has gone into hibernation, and now finally even my brain is whacked!!

Alas!! If only I'd listened to the doctor and made do with watered wine!

And now it's too late! Maro! Maro! Lead me to the hospital for crackpots!'

'Naso! Listen, it's me! It's me, Maro! I've metamorphosed into a refrigerator! Are you listening to me?'

'Oh, it's the end! This is definitely the end!!

It sounds to me as if this refrigerator is speaking in a voice just like that of my dear old pal Virgil!! Alas and alack!!!'

Returning to his place under the sofa, Ovid put his head to the floor and began sobbing desperately, paying no heed at all to anything I said.

There was nothing else for me to do, so I came here."

"If I woke up to find myself transformed into a refrigerator, I think it's extremely unlikely that I'd be able to remain as calm as you've been."

"No matter what happens to you, no matter how strong the passions you find yourself experiencing, you have to be able to keep it all under control if you're going to be a true poet. For the poet, the Self is the first Other, right? Am I wrong?"

The refrigerator flashed me a grin.

Sipping a couple of beers that Virgil had bought and cooled off inside himself on his way to "The Poetry School," the two of us continued our colloquy.

"Ah, it's nice and cold."

"Yup. I seem to work pretty well as a refrigerator."

"Have you any thoughts regarding the reasons for your metamorphosis?"

"None at all. The very idea of calling this a metamorphosis strikes me as . . . well, back when I was young people used to metamorphose into swans and such—I'm sure you're familiar with Leda's case—but that was about it. In those days, metamorphoses were always highly elegant affairs."

"Lately people have started metamorphosing into vermin and enormous breasts and things like that. Times have changed."

"I rather doubt that such cases can even be termed metamorphoses in the strict sense. Take the instance of the guy who turned into a big bug. His case might be explained as a sudden retrogressive alteration in genetic sequence brought about by cosmic rays or something along those lines. You could say that, as a result of this genetic transformation, he simply dropped down a few branches on the tree of evolution—it's just that it happened very suddenly, within the space of a single night.

As for the incident of the man who metamorphosed into an enormous breast, medical research has shown that it was due to a rapid increase in hormonal levels spurred by certain abnormalities in the subject's endocrine glands.

I think it's much harder to rationally explain why people would turn into werewolves on the night of the full moon. Metamorphoses of that sort are more up Ovid's aisle, I suppose. Another beer, honored bard?"

"No thanks, Virgil. None for me."

"Call me Maro. Well, then, what could have made me metamorphose into a fridge?"

I was thinking.

About metamorphosing into a refrigerator. About Virgil. About the fate of poets in this world of ours.

"Maro, could you pass me another beer?"

"That's the way to be, honored bard! I got cheese in here, too, if you want it."

I drank his beer. Can after can after can. And Virgil the Fridge joined me in gulping down can after can after can.

"Hey, Maro."

"What's on your mind, young but honored bard?"

"I think there may be a psychological explanation."

"Ah? And how would that go? You want another beer?"

"Thanks. See, the way I figure it, you're what you'd call a very rigid classicist; as such, you wanted to keep everything frozen, preserved just as it was. That makes sense, right? That urge was always a part of your deeper psychological makeup, but when it came into contact with Ovid it erupted. How's that?"

"Well, it does hold together, it's true. And it has a kind of simple beauty, sort of like a can of beer that's gone flat. Oh dear, oh dear—don't think I meant that as an insult or anything, because I didn't. Shall I tell you my own hypothesis?"

"Please."

"The poet's deeper psychological makeup contained a second urge entirely different from the one you mentioned.

A poet is always aiming to commit the perfect crime. But what, you ask, is this perfect crime? It is to create an entirely indecipherable work of art, of course. And the refrigerator is simply a refrigerator. It's damn near impossible to find any sort of meaning or thought in a refrigerator. On the other hand, vermin, breasts . . . please, it's too obvious.

Thus the mature poet channeled every ounce of his gift into the great plan: his murder in a sealed room. And this work of art—it was the refrigerator. How does that strike you?"

"It's amazing."

Virgil and I drank and drank and drank.

Virgil never lost control of himself, no matter how much he drank.

"Excuse me, I'll be back in a moment."

"Eh? Whither are you headed?"

"I've got to take a piss. You're okay, Maro?"

"Apparently those coils on my back turn it into steam and it just disperses into the air. Frankly, it's not bad being a refrigerator."

I was so tired, so very tired, so very very tired, so very very very tired, so very very very very tired that I could no longer resist. Here Virgil had made this special trip just to come and see me, and I had gotten so tired I simply couldn't manage to keep myself awake.

My head sank down onto the desk and stayed there. Way off in the distance, I heard the sounds of Virgil gathering up the empty cans and putting them inside "himself."

"Maro. Hey, Maro."

"Yes? What is it?"

"I'm so sorry. I wasn't any help at all."

"Don't be silly. It was fun talking with you, young but honored bard."

"Maro. Hey, Maro, what are you going to do now?"

"Young but honored bard, what do you think?"

"You're a refrigerator, Maro."

"Is that all?"

"You're a poet, Maro."

"And what do poets do?"

"They write poems."

"Exactly. Until now I've been a poet for people. Henceforth I will be a poet for refrigerators. How's that strike you?"

"That's wonderful, Maro."

"If you don't mind, there's one thing I want to ask you."

"Go right ahead."

"The word 'refrigerator' is absent from both Ancient Greek and Latin. Since the word doesn't exist, there are no words with which it rhymes. I'm the sort of poet who can't write without end rhymes. Do you think maybe you could give me a word that rhymes with it in English?"

"Sure thing, Maro. It rhymes with *alligator*."

"Ah, that's a nice rhyme. Yes, I like that a lot."

By now I was almost asleep.

"Sayonara," said the refrigerator.

Sayonara, I burped in reply.

Sayonara, Virgil.

Sayonara, Maro.

Sayonara, refrigerator.

Listening to the medley of sounds that the great ancestor of all poets, born in the year seventy B.C.—the great Virgil, illustrious refrigerator—made as he opened the door and padded quietly away up the stairs . . . I closed my eyes.

6.

No sooner had "Some Incomprehensible Thing" entered the classroom than it expanded to fill the entire space and began screaming.

"Some Incomprehensible Thing" had no shape, no color, no weight, and no odor; it just hung about expanding, contracting, and whirlpooling into itself.

"Take a seat in that chair," I said.

I wasn't at all sure that "Some Incomprehensible Thing" understood human speech, but then I wasn't at all sure that it didn't either.

"Please be seated!!"

But "Some Incomprehensible Thing" remained plastered across the ceiling, swaying slowly back and forth and side to side.

I gave it one last warning.

"You are to sit down immediately! There will be no class unless you sit down. That's the rule here. Sit!"

Replying to my order with an "Okay," "Some Incomprehensible Thing" drifted/oozed/fluttered/galumphed down from the ceiling.

"Some Incomprehensible Thing" was making an earnest attempt to seat itself in the chair, but before two seconds had elapsed it started drooping downwards to the floor, and by the time a further three seconds had passed it was cascading in a landslide off the chair.

"All right," I said, as "Some Incomprehensible Thing" assumed a stringy form and began trying desperately to bind itself to the chair, looking as if it had made up its mind to sit on the damn thing if it was the last thing it ever did. "All right, it's okay, you don't have to sit down if you can't manage it. I take back what I said earlier. Please assume whatever position is comfortable."

After a number of different attempts, "Some Incomprehensible Thing" finally managed to affix itself to the chair by tying itself into a Nanking knot.

"Sorry to keep you waiting," said "Some Incomprehensible Thing."

"What am I, do you think?" asked "Some Incomprehensible Thing."

Bingo! I thought. I'd had a feeling it was going to say that. Things of this nature always ask you what they are. As if I'd have any idea! How on earth should I know when the things themselves are unable to figure it out?

"In principle, I think that's something you should figure out yourself," I said.

"Some Incomprehensible Thing" began to squirm about, endeavoring to untie its knot.

"What's up? Is something wrong?"

"I'm leaving! What a sham! I can see my hopes were misplaced."

"Some Incomprehensible Thing" kept struggling to untie its knot, but only succeeded in getting itself more and more entangled.

"Would you like me to give you a hand?"

"Keep your hands off me!"

"I think if you . . ."

"Stop distracting me!! Just keep quiet!!"

"Some Incomprehensible Thing" was foundering. The poor thing had started to realize that its own actions were utterly incomprehensible to itself.

The chair looked as if it hadn't quite understood the seriousness of the situation unfolding around it. It kept twisting ticklishly this way and that.

"Oh, what a mess!" bewailed "Some Incomprehensible Thing." "Please help me, Mr. Teacher! Get me out of this!"

"Some Incomprehensible Thing" pleaded in its now enfeebled voice for me to effect its rescue.

I inspected the chair, then inspected "Some Incomprehensible Thing," now fifth-dimensionally welded to various points on the chair's surface.

"Do you think you can help me, Mr. Teacher?"

"I'm afraid it's hopeless. You and this chair will be together until the end of the world."

"Some Incomprehensible Thing" burst into tears.

"What! But how can that be! Oh-h-h-h!"

I left "Some Incomprehensible Thing" alone for some time, while it sobbed and wailed, until finally it ran out of tears.

And then it was time! Discerning that "Some Incomprehensible Thing" had wept itself into a state of total fatigue, I smiled and hailed it joyously.

"Congratulations! Well done!"

"Huh? What did you say?"

"Some Incomprehensible Thing" thought it had misheard.

"Congratulations! You've finally managed to figure out what you are, right? Am I correct? I'm sure you must have understood by now."

"Yeah . . . well . . . I guess I kind of figured . . . so . . . what am I, then?"

"You're a CHAIR-LIKE ENTITY. The whole purpose of your existence was to join up with that chair."

"Oh, I knew it! That's just what I was thinking myself!"

"Some Incomprehensible Thing" told me how delighted it was to have discovered what it was, and said that while it realized it was a terribly audacious request to make, it hoped I might consent to let it take the chair away with it.

Oh, by all means. How could I possibly object?

"Go right ahead, please. The chair is practically a part of you, after all."

"Some Incomprehensible Thing" went off in a splendid mood, basking in the newfound knowledge that it was a chair-like entity, and I started sweeping the floor. I was still sweeping when I came across a little fragment of "Some Incomprehensible Thing" that "Some Incomprehensible Thing" had left behind when it departed.

It was nothing but a strange little lump that fluttered/ swung/squelched.

After just a moment's thought, I tossed the swinging/ squelching tad into the trash.

Actually, I have no idea what "Some Incomprehensible Thing" was.

7.

I want you to imagine an average man.
A man average in all respects.
He's somewhere between 37 and 40 years old. Height between five foot three and five foot five. Four cavities. Glasses with dark-brown frames, correction in the lenses for a slight astigmatism. Two children. The older one, a girl, is in eighth grade—she's just had her first period. She started pretty late compared to other girls these days, and apparently she had been agonizing over the matter for some time. Well, well, glad things have turned out all right. The younger child is a boy in fourth grade, the sort of kid who's constantly getting caught up in something or other. A craze for building models was just the first of many. Sherman tanks, remote-controlled doodads, stamps, coins, pennants, video-game baseball, baseball, soccer, the fan club of somebody or other, The Enter to Win Coca-Cola Quiz, phone-in requests to the radio, imitations of cartoon characters' voices . . . and yet for some strange reason the boy simply refuses to pick up a book.

A wife who appears to be somewhere between 33 and 38 with a contraceptive ring implanted in the neck of her uterus. Her sexual appetite is so voracious it's both wondrous and frightening. She says she read in a magazine that it's not injurious to her health to have sex during her periods.

He'd like to keep his smoking down to no more than 10 cigarettes a day. He would rather not end up with lung cancer. He would like to have at least two extra-marital affairs before he dies. The prospect of spending the rest of his life having sex with no one but his present wife is just too bleak. One affair will be with an office worker under his command, a young lassie between the ages of 17 and 18, let's say. No, hold on. He'd better give that one some thought. What if he were her first lover—things could get messy if the girl got too swept up in the relationship. Things could get really messy. It's supposed to be a casual fling at the most, one or two encounters and that's it—he certainly doesn't want to end up getting demoted or have his wife walk out on him just for that.

It's not easy being average.

The average man placed a business card in front of me.

> **JOVIAN**
> **(MAN FROM JUPITER)**

I flipped the card over.

> **Don't be lonely! I'll be your friend**
> **For the night. Call me.**
> **♥ 000-1111**

"What exactly made you have this card printed?" I asked the **JOVIAN** posing as the average man.

The **JOVIAN** told me he had been taught that the

average man always carried a business card, and did I mean to say this information had been incorrect?

I informed him that while the front side certainly resembled the business cards that average men carry on their person, the style of the reverse side resembled the cards used by unaverage women in their dealings with average men, and observed that it was highly undesirable to mix these two styles.

"And I wonder," I went on, "if the positive effects which accrue from your going to the trouble of posing as an earthling aren't wholly undermined by the fact that you have the word **JOVIAN** printed on your card? See what I mean?"

The **JOVIAN** rose swiftly to his feet.

I thought I was the spitting image of the average man. You think I'm not?

Your image is perfect, it's true—but then the business card is part of the image. If you want to pose as an earthling, it's essential that you learn to master these little agreed-upon niceties, I explained.

Earthling thought processes make no sense, sighed the **JOVIAN**.

"And what was your reason for coming here?"

I came here from Jupiter on vacation—getting the look right was hard enough, of course, but gadzooks did I suffer with the language! We have no language on Jupiter, dear sir, and so I was thoroughly at a loss, most bewildered—and though I managed to acquire enough of a grasp of earthspeech that I can handle everyday exchanges without difficulty, earthspeech is unsuited to explaining the way things are on Jupiter—I'm worried that my amicable relations with earthlings may be undermined—therefore I would be grateful if you could teach me how to use earthspeech in as Jovian a manner as possible, said the **JOVIAN** politely, and held out a form on which was printed the word "Receipt."

Sign here, please.

I informed the **JOVIAN** that the situation did not call for a "Receipt," and he withdrew it with an expression that made it plain he was dissatisfied.

The **JOVIAN** picked up a piece of chalk and set about expounding the dissonances that arose when earthspeech collided with Jovian concepts, writing out his examples on the blackboard.

Example 1   A phenomenon equivalent to that expressed by the earthword "time" is found on Jupiter as well, but for some unintelligible reason earthlings only recognize the following four separate varieties of "time."

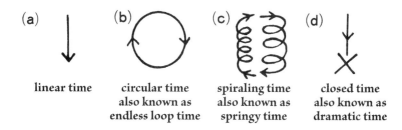

(a) linear time

(b) circular time
also known as
endless loop time

(c) spiraling time
also known as
springy time

(d) closed time
also known as
dramatic time

On Jupiter, in addition to types (a) (b) (c) and (d) above, we also recognize a large number of fixed-quantity "times," such as "single wave time," "cycloid curve time," "geoid curve time," "catastrophic time," "Planck's constant time," and "Dirac-type time"; in addition, we have "times" whose quantity is not fixed.

" 'Times' whose quantity isn't fixed? What's that?"

Note to Example 1. A "time" whose quantity is not fixed is an anti-effective temporal phenomenon that arises in the direction that cancels changes in some "time" whose quantity is fixed—among the terms available to one compelled to explain in earthspeech, those which appear most similar are "laugh time," "chat time," "drink-like-a-fish time," and so on.

For instance, in Jovian terms "time's a big laugh" indicates that something is extremely sad.

Example 2 A phenomenon equivalent to that expressed by the earthword "death" is found on Jupiter as well, but for some unintelligible reason earthlings have only the following three kinds of "death":

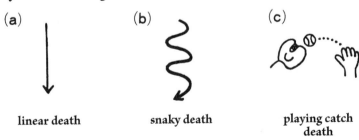

| (a) | (b) | (c) |
| linear death | snaky death | playing catch death |

Without even realizing it, I gasped.

"What! But there's only one kind of 'death' on earth!"

Note to Example 2. Being a Jovian, I am unable to acquire a firm grasp of the finer points of this matter, but doesn't it seem plausible that originally there were three separate, distinct words in earthspeech for "death" and that, over time, these gradually merged to become a single word? Because the fact of the matter is, earthling deaths occur in these three different ways.

On Jupiter today, we have types (a) and (b) above, but type (c) doesn't exist. There are extremely few places in the universe where type (c) "playing catch death" is practiced. On Jupiter, we have another type known as "jumping death," but it is highly ceremonial and only on extremely rare occasions does one have the opportunity to witness it firsthand.

Example 3   A distinction roughly equivalent to that indicated by the earthwords "sex" and "gender" is found on Jupiter as well, but for some unintelligible reason earthlings have an array of five different "sexes" or "genders," namely:

(a) "male-male" man
(b) "male-male" woman
(c) "male-female" woman
(d) "female-male" woman
(e) "female-female" woman

On Jupiter we only distinguish between "men" and "women."

I considered interrupting him at this point, but the JOVIAN was so overweeningly confident of the truth of what he was saying that I decided to keep quiet.

Example 4 A phenomenon equivalent to that expressed by the earthword "beauty" is found on Jupiter as well. In fact, there are seven different kinds of "beauty" on Jupiter. Why, then, is there no "beauty" on earth?

I find it exceedingly regrettable that only the word has survived. Perhaps this, too, is a case of gradual extinction.

I voiced assent.

Example 5 As for the earthword "God," I find it unintelligible that such a word should have been created when no such being has ever existed here on earth. Of course, "God" does exist on Jupiter—perhaps the "God" of whom earthlings speak is really the Jovian "God," discovered by them while it was on vacation.

"So there really is a God on Jupiter?"

Note to Example 5. Swarms of them, actually.

"It seems to me that the speech we earthlings use has yet to develop to the point where we can express concepts found in your Jovian world. I would thus suggest—and this is only a suggestion—that you be a good sport and give up on the whole idea, granting the puerile earth languages a reprieve of some length of time . . . of **(a) linear time**, I mean to say . . . in which to mature. There is no doubt in my mind that given another 40 or 50 thousand years, our earth languages, nothing but buds at present, will have grown up and turned into beautiful women, women like enormous blossoms. You'll find it impossible to return things to their former state if, in attempting to force the puerile earth languages to express Jovian concepts, you send them into a state of shock—what the Germans call *Trauma*."

The **SATURNIANS** refer to words in a state of *Trauma* as "nutcase words" and are much enamored of them, so that whenever a new little word is born to the world, its parents make it watch loads of horror movies, and tell it that as a matter of fact it isn't their child at all, they picked it up on **PLUTO**, and do everything else they can to turn it into a "nutcase word"—how about that?—personally, I think that would be a much speedier solution, said the **JOVIAN**.

I allowed my tone to turn slightly nasty.

"Earth languages exist in order to express the concepts of earthlings. They do not exist for you and your buddies."

I'm sorry, I shouldn't have said that, said the **JOVIAN**.

We **JOVIANS** are just as firmly opposed to child abuse as you earthlings—with your permission, I will wait until my next vacation to have the pleasure of hearing earth languages express our **JOVIAN** concepts.

"I'm glad you've understood," I said.

The **JOVIAN** stuck out the pinky of his right hand.

PINKY SWEAR!, said the **JOVIAN**.

8.

The guard was in agony over his profession. He suffered *pangs of conscience.* Or to put it in more nearly accurate terms, the guard felt *a craving for the truth.*

"For a long time I never even dreamed anything suspicious was happening. It's embarrassing. I think my analytic capacity must have been very poor."

Everything begins in doubt.

"I was making the rounds. It was the middle of the night. I was opening the observation slots, making my inspection just like always. And then, suddenly, *it* struck me. Man oh man, was I surprised. But why hadn't *it* ever occurred to me before? I just couldn't understand. Oh god, it was awful to realize how long it had taken me to notice—so awful it brought tears to my eyes, seriously."

The guard had started wondering *why on earth he had been going around all this time believing that the place where he worked was a prison.*

"I think I must have been off my rocker since birth."

The guard tried to figure out what sort of place he was working at. He thought about the nature of his work. About the size of his salary. About the attitude the guests assumed in their dealings with him. And having considered the various possibilities, he came to the conclusion that his place of work must be either one of the following:

(1) A hospital

(2) A hotel

Only he was unable to say which it was. He had nothing to go by.

"If the answer is (1), I'm a nurse.

If the answer is (2), I'm a bellboy.

But either way, I'm certainly not a guard."

Since the guard was not a "guard," from now on I will call him "the man."

No objections, I take it?

"None," replied the man.

In Room 1 there were a man and a woman. The man was a spy from the CIA who had infiltrated the KGB. The woman was a spy from the KGB who had infiltrated the CIA. After infiltrating the Chinese Ministry of National Defense through separate routes, the two of them had fallen in love. The KGB, the CIA, and the Chinese Ministry of National Defense had sent out agents to track them down, but thanks to all the assistance the two received from the KGB, the CIA, and the Chinese Ministry of Defense, they had managed to shake these agents off.

They hope the misunderstandings will be cleared up soon.

If only these misunderstandings could be cleared up, the two of them could go around spying together, happy as two lovebirds.

The man shares their hope that the misunderstandings

will be cleared up soon, because he thinks it would be really nice if the two of them could return again to the glamorous world of espionage they have left behind.

Room 2. An old lady was being held here. Or was she just living here?

"She's *planted* there," said the man. The old lady's name was Tatum O'Neil, otherwise known as T.O. One of these old ladies who seem to have been around since before the dawn of history. As a matter of fact, before the dawn of history she worked as a hostess at a sex parlor, and was very skilled at the job.

"You know, I was written up in a novel once," the old lady would say. "Only the book didn't make any sort of splash at all, and the author got so dispirited that he ate too much cheesecake and died."

The old lady had been rooted in Room 2 since before the man was born.

"If you have any sexual troubles or doubts or anything, don't hesitate to ask me for advice. I'd be glad to teach you the theory. Mind you, I won't go any further than that," the old lady would say.

The man really liked talking with the nice, nice, old, old lady.

Smoke was billowing from Room 3. The man rushed to open the door. This is how it always was. These people were simply too much. They had built a big bonfire in the middle of the room, and they were sitting in a big circle around it playing the guitar and singing folk songs.

Yes the da-a-a-wn's draw-wing near!!

Yes the da-a-a-wn's draw-wing near!!

Sheesh, talk about singing out of tune! Keep on like that and even that dawn of yours will start having second thoughts, people. After scooping up a bucketful of water and putting out the fire, the man ordered the totally-lacking-in-common-sense screwballs to give the room a good cleaning, pronto.

"Chill out, man, we'll clean, we'll clean. Man, what a racket!"

There's this one young woman who's completely stoned. Her waist has gotten so gelatinous she can't even stand.

The girl turns to the man and calls out glumly, "Hey, you the guard?"

Ah, poor thing's done too much drugs, she's gone totally bonkers, thinks the man. She gets it into her head that I'm a *guard*, of all things.

"Yeah, that's right, I'm the guard. So you'd better listen to what I say, okay? And I say you just keep sitting there, nice and easy."

The girl does keep sitting there, glum as ever.

I bet she's actually a nice girl, thinks the man. She's just gone bonkers.

In Room 4, there was a little boy about six years old.

The little boy had on a pair of shorts, and he sat in his chair with his "My Little Sketchpad" lying open on the desk in front of him, totally absorbed in the picture he was drawing with his pencils. There was a yellow ribbon pinned to the short-sleeved button-down shirt he wore. The man had absolutely no idea what the "yellow ribbon" meant.

The man is not well-versed in the ways of the world.

"Howdy," says the man.

"Hello. Look, it's a *giraffe.*"

The little boy shows the man the "giraffe" he's drawn. When the man first caught sight of it, he was impressed that a little boy of six could do such a good job drawing an "ostrich." Looking more closely, he notices two vaguely leg-like objects protruding from the area around its chest.

The little boy turns the page.

Ah . . . I bet it's a "duck," thinks the man.

"It's an *elephant,*" says the little boy.

Ah . . . I bet it's a "crow," thinks the man.

"It's a *hamadryad baboon,*" says the little boy.

Ah . . . I bet it's a "tulip." No, wait . . . I bet they're "basketball shoes." No, no, hold on a second . . . I bet it's a "helicopter."

"This one is *you.* Doesn't it look like you?"

"Oh yes, just like me!" says the man.

The little boy tears out a sheet of paper and hands it to the man.

"For the girl next door," says the little boy. It's against the rules, but since it's such a trifling matter the man prefers just to keep quiet and look the other way. He wishes the boy's room could be a little bigger and a little brighter, too.

The little girl in Room 5 was playing house. She had three dolls.

"This is 'Anne.' She's the oldest, and she's eight years old. This one is 'Betty.' She's only five, but she's very precocious. And this is 'Bobby.' 'Bobby' hasn't been born yet, so he doesn't speak very well."

The little girl has "Betty" watch over "Bobby" while "Anne" prepares dinner.

" 'Oh "Anne"! "Bobby" is crying! Could he be hungry?'

'No, "Betty"! When he cries like that, it means he's sleepy.'

'Weeaaaaah, weeaaaaah.'

'Oh "Anne"! "Bobby" won't stop crying! What should I do?'

'Listen "Betty"! When he cries like that you need to *change his diaper.'* "

"So tell me, 'Betty,' where's your daddy?" asks the man.

" 'Daddy just evaporated into thin air one day.' "

"Tell me, 'Anne,' where's your mommy?'

" 'Mommy seems to have run off with some man.' "

"Tell me, 'Bobby,' where's your grandpa?"

" 'Oh, he killed grandma, so he had to go to jail.' "

"Here, it's from your neighbor."

The man gives the little girl in Room 5 the picture from the little boy in Room 4.

This one is a picture of a "carrot." No . . . I bet it's a "radish." Wait, I bet it's "celery." Or maybe it's a "tennis racquet"?

Well, I'll prepare myself so that I'm not startled even if she tells me it's "Eisenhower," thinks the man. *I'm obviously a total novice where pictures are concerned.*

"What do you think this is a picture of?" asks the man.

The little girl makes a strange face. She doesn't get what the man is saying.

"It's a carrot. I think it's wonderfully drawn. I think it must be terribly difficult to draw a carrot as skillfully as this. I'd love to meet this little boy. Do you think maybe someday I'll be able to meet him?"

Of course you'll be able to meet him. It's not like this is a prison or anything.

"Sooner or later I'll take you to see him, I promise," says the man.

" 'Oh, I'm glad!' " says "Betty."

" 'Oh, I'm glad!' " says "Anne."

" 'Boy oh boy, am I glad!' " says "Bobby."

The man doesn't like Room 6. Listening to the manic-depressive kangaroo go on and on about bygone days makes the man feel as if he were going to turn manic-depressive himself. The schizophrenic stork who had the room before the kangaroo was so much calmer, the man thinks, and the stork had class, too.

Room 7.

"What's wrong?" I asked.

The man was completely out of sorts.

"There's no way it could be a hospital or a hotel, either one. I was forgetting. There's a desert in Room 7. I lost track of where the exit was once and ended up wandering around in there for three days. If I'd been inside much longer I would have starved to death. I mean, there's no way either a hospital or a hotel would have a desert inside, is there? That's ridiculous, right?"

The man's shoulders slumped and his head sagged.

"Do you like your job?" I asked.

"Yeah, I like it okay."

"And how are the guests?"

"Some of them can be difficult, but most are very nice."

"I'm afraid I can't tell you what your job is. However, I think I can say with a fair amount of confidence that I do understand the pain of not knowing what one's job is. I know it's hard, but I really think that it'd be better for you not to do anything drastic, not to rush things. You yourself know more than anyone else about your job. No one else can help you as far as that's concerned. And that holds true for me as well. There's nothing you can do but continue to work just as you have up to now, and to go on thinking just as you have up to now. I'm afraid that's all I can tell you."

"I see," responded the man. "I'll give it a try. But *how* am I to think?"

As the man stood up to leave, I gave him my two bits.

"You should think with your heart," I said.

"Think with my heart, you say?"

The man went back to his place of work.

9.

The students have all left.

I'm sitting alone in the "classroom" now, thinking back over the day's classes.

Did I attempt to force my values or my aesthetics on the students?

Did I remain patient with the students at all times?

Did I shout at the students that their use of language was bizarre?

Did I behave towards the students as if I knew everything?

Did I walk hand in hand with the students to a point just one step short of "poetry," making no false steps along the way?

There was still some "Song Book Blend" left, so I drank it.

The lights went out.

The classroom was completely dark.

10.

Sitting there in the perfect darkness of "The Poetry School," I started thinking about the poems that our students are eventually bound to write.

Some of those poems will be beautiful, and simple, and strong. And some will be ugly and confused.

Among them there will be some that are weird, some that are kind of gross, some that are dimwitted, some that are really rather monstrous, some that are sad, some that are infantile, some that are funny, some that are so ridiculous you can hardly bear to read them, some that stick to the rules, some that don't stick to the rules, some that simply don't know that there are rules, some that are embarrassed, some that lie, and some that are pretentious.

Among them there will be everything in the world but good poems.

I got to my feet and groped my way out of the classroom.

11.

Song Book sat dozing in the rocking chair, shrouded in her yellow muumuu, her legs sticking straight out. "Henry IV" had imbibed and gotten a trifle bit high, and was weaving aimlessly around her feet.

"Nee-yow, nee-yow," cried "Henry IV." He'd meant to say "Mee-ow," but it was coming out as "Nee-yow" because he was drunk.

"Be quiet, will you? And how about cutting down on the booze? It'll be too late once you end up an alcoholic, you know."

"Henry IV" pretended not to understand what I was saying, and started letting loose a series of "Mooo, mooo"s. Cow imitation was "Henry IV" 's star gag.

Assuming a bullish head-to-the-ground position and continuing to unleash his "Mooo, mooo"s, "Henry IV" began charging my feet.

I put "Henry IV" under arrest and threw him in the slammer of his basket.

For some time after I shut the lid on him, "Henry IV" continued to yell out at me from inside, raising his voice in bellows of displeasure such as "Mooo, mooo" and "Woof, woof" and "Cockledoodledoo." Then, all of a sudden, "Henry IV" fell asleep and started snoring.

I opened the lid of the basket.

"Sorry," I said.

It was a cruel thing to have done. Really, if I were "Henry IV" and obsessed with the notion that my mother and my siblings had all died as a direct result of my birth, I seriously doubt whether events would have played themselves out in as harmless a manner as getting pie-eyed and yelling "Mooo, mooo" while charging into battle against my master's feet.

12.

I walked over to the snoozing Song Book.
Her legs were aligned, sticking out perfectly straight.
Her hands were arranged neatly on her knees.
An open comic book lay under her hands.
Song Book makes no effort to follow the story when it comes to comic books. Song Book just likes looking through them, jumping from scene to scene. She goes on gazing for ages at scenes she likes. That's how she reads comics.
Song Book falls asleep gazing at her favorite scenes.
I gazed gently down over Song Book's shoulder at the scene unfolding beneath her hands.

13.

I gazed at Song Book as she slept.

14.

I laid a hand on hers. Because I wanted Song Book to know I was *here*.

Slowly, very slowly, Song Book awoke.
First she noticed my hand, then she noticed my suit and my socks, and finally, after a long, long time, she noticed me.
"Oh," said Song Book, very quietly.

"Welcome home."

15.

I dislike difficult words.

When I read something that's been written using difficult words, I get very sad. I mean, it's so hard to understand what it all means.

I dislike difficult words, yet from time to time I use them. God, is that sad.

I like the words "Welcome home."

I like the "Welcome home" Song Book says to me when I come home at night.

I'm not familiar with other "Welcome home"s.

I lift Song Book up from the rocking chair and carry her to bed.

"You sure are heavy, aren't you?"

"Good night," said Song Book.

Then I turned out the light.

16.

I was reading to "Henry IV" from Eric Routley's "The Puritan Pleasures of the Detective Story."

"'Our twentieth century might be likened to a "steel man," enclosed in a shell of materialism, shiny and hard. This man of steel will perish, too, through having failed to realize that his deceptively solid armor has deprived of air a soul that needs more than words and ideas as nourishment.

Never have human eyes been as avid as they are today; never have they searched so desperately; for art has been removed from them. The lamentable misunderstanding fostered by the sordid misconceptions of the nineteenth-century middle classes has led art into a kind of suicide. Reacting against the middle class pursuit of profit, and attempting to restore art to health, the modern mystery novel has lost contact with the public and shut itself off within the closed circle of its own eccentricities.

As a result the detective story has become a technique applied to particular means; it has lost the sense of its function and become an infinitely rarefied form of play for specialists, for mandarins who scorn human society and take refuge, as though on a desert island, in a solitary concern with themselves and their own intellectual virtuosity.

The appeal sent forth by Raymond Chandler cuts across the whole history of the mystery novel, and has broken down the walls erected by aesthetic theory; that is why, no doubt, it is heard by so many today, even though they do not clearly comprehend its significance. In the face of those who remain deaf to his cry, Chandler proclaims the enduring human role of art, a role to which it is entitled, and which we are entitled to have it fill. Assailed by images, but deprived of their natural aid, modern man is moving toward a crisis the nature of which can be easily foreseen.' "

Suddenly "Henry IV" pricked up his ears.

It was the doorbell ringing.

"Someone's come," yelled Song Book in the kitchen.

I put the book down and went to the door.

"Who's there?"

There was no reply.

I opened the door.

Four gangsters stood on the doorstep.

Part Three:
Sayonara, Gangsters

I "I'm so sorry"

1.

There were four gangsters, as advertised on the Most Wanted poster.

Everyone, each and every one of us, knew their names.

"The Mute Gangster" stepped into the room, his lips tightly clamped together.

"The Short Gangster" stepped into the room, toting his machine gun and telling us that if we knew what was good for us we'd keep our traps shut.

"The Fat Gangster" stepped into the room, licking his lollipop and apologizing for the inconvenient intrusion.

Last of all, "The Beautiful Gangster" stepped into the room.

Song Book clutched my hand in hers, keeping her trap shut.

"We'd like to have a class in poetry," said "The Beautiful Gangster."

"What, you mean here?"

"Yes."

I turned to Song Book.

"I'll be holding a class here. Prepare a blackboard and chairs."

2.

"Good evening, everyone," I said. "Before we get started, there's one small matter I'd like to clear up, which is that if you've dropped by on us with the intention of committing a robbery, you're in the wrong place. We lack valuables."

"No shit, Sherlock. What kind of idiots would hit a measly joint like yours?" said "The Short Gangster." "We ain't here to burgle, buddy."

"I see what you mean."

I stood and picked up a piece of chalk.

"Hold it right there!" shouted "The Short Gangster."

"The Short Gangster" aimed his machine gun right at my heart.

"What's that thing you got?" he asked.

"It's a piece of chalk."

"And what're you planning to do with it?"

"I thought I might teach this class."

"With a piece of chalk?"

"Yes."

"Lemme take a look at that piece of chalk. Don't throw it, man! Hand it to me. As soon as you've passed it over, you put both hands up over your head."

Pinching the chalk, "The Short Gangster" shook it delicately back and forth. Then "The Short Gangster" snapped it in two.

"This stuff inside—it's chalk, too?"

"That's right."

"And what are you gonna do with this thing?"

"I'm going to teach the class."

"What exactly do you mean when you say 'class'?"

"It's a little difficult to explain."

"You trying to lie to us?"

"Not at all."

"All right, then. What's this class thing you keep gabbing about?"

"It's when you get together and think about the truth."

"That's it? You just think?"

"You think very hard."

"Yeah, okay. And where does that get you?"

"It doesn't get you anywhere."

"So, thinking about stuff that gets you nowhere, that's class?"

"Yeah, pretty much."

"And you're telling me that's your job?"

"That's right."

"Cheeky bastard! You know what that is? That's racketeering, bub."

"I don't disagree with you there."

"What did you say you think about?"

"The truth."

"Explain that one to me."

"It's sort of difficult to put it into words."

"You wanna die, is that it? Don't mess with me, bud!"

Without getting up from his chair, "The Short Gangster" placed his teensy little finger on the trigger of his machine gun.

"The truth about poetry, that's what I mean. That's all I

deal with here."

"Should have said so from the beginning, then, huh? And what's that?"

"I'm afraid I don't understand it very well myself."

"You're telling me you spend your time thinking very hard about something you don't understand very well and that doesn't get you anywhere?"

"Yes."

"And you take money for that?"

"Yes."

"You know what people like you are called?"

"No."

"Petty thieves. We don't do stuff like that."

"I'm terribly ashamed of myself."

"Whatever, let it drop. Now tell me, what are you gonna teach *us*?"

"Oh, you know. Nothing much."

"What's this I've got here?"

"It's a machine gun."

"What happens when I pull the trigger?"

"It shoots a bullet."

"It'll hurt like hell when it hits you. Catch my drift?"

"I think so."

"I'll ask you again. Ready? What are you gonna teach *us*?"

"I'm going to teach you how to write poems."

"And what good will that do us?"

"I'm afraid its practical value is rather negligible."

"You're telling me it's not gonna do us any good at all?"

"I'm not sure I would go that far."

"Teach us well if you value your life, bud. Got that?"

"I think so."

"Okay, then, get busy!"

3.

I turned to "The Mute Gangster."

"Stand up, please. I mean, if you wouldn't mind."

Heaving himself sluggishly to his feet, "The Mute Gangster" placed a hand on the Luger automatic he carried in the holster at his hip. All his preparations were now complete: he could blow me away at a moment's notice.

"Talk to me about what's going through your mind. Just take whatever it is you're thinking right now, whatever it is you're feeling, and turn it into words. It doesn't matter what it is. Don't rush yourself, try to keep calm, and talk slowly," I said.

"The Mute Gangster" stood there, his lips just as tightly clamped shut as ever, looking as if he had never ever opened them except to dump in coffee and sandwiches.

"The Mute Gangster" peered at my face from under the brim of his floppy felt hat, his expression filled with sadness. His expression seemed to say, *I'm not so good at thinking about things that aren't coffee and sandwiches.*

"It doesn't have to be hard," I said. "Say what you like."

"The Mute Gangster" began hunting around for some kind of word, any word he could find written down on any page in his head, but all his pages were blank.

Blank. Blank. Blank. Blank.

Blank. Blank. Blank. Blank.

At long last a few solemn syllables spilled from the lips of "The Mute Gangster."

"Coffee and sandwiches."

"All right, great, you're doing fine. Keep going."

Blank. Blank. Blank. Blank.

Blank. Blank. Blank. Blank.

"The Mute Gangster" whispered the same words again, very sadly.

"Coffee and sandwiches."

The remaining three gangsters gazed in awe at the lips of "The Mute Gangster."

Blank. Blank. Blank. Blank.

Blank. And then, yet again—

"Coffee and . . ." whispered "The Mute Gangster."

He fell silent. "The Mute Gangster," as if to chase off the phantom of "coffee and sandwiches" that haunted him, waved a hand through the air.

"The Mute Gangster" was groping for some other word, any word other than "coffee and sandwiches" that played a role in his life.

Blank. Blank. Blank. Blank.

Blank. Blank. Blank. Blank.

Blank. Blank. Blank. Blank.

"The Mute Gangster" 's face went pale, and sweat beaded on his forehead.

Blank. Blank. Blank. Blank.

Blank. Blank. Blank. Blank.

"*Baby*," groaned "The Mute Gangster."

"Splendid!" I cried. "Keep trying!"

Blank. Blank. Blank. Blank.

Blank. Blank. Blank. Blank.

Blank. Blank. Blank. Blank.

"Earwax," muttered "The Mute Gangster." His shoulders heaved with a sigh.

Blank. Blank. Blank. Blank.
Blank. Blank. Blank. Blank.
Blank. Blank. Blank. Blank.
Blank. Blank. Blank. Blank.
"Nosebleed!!!"

Tears shone in "The Mute Gangster" 's eyes. They were tears of despair.

"Take it slowly," I said. "Take your time, keep hunting. No need to hurry."

Blank. Blank. Blank. Blank.
Blank. Blank. Blank. Blank.
Blank. Blank. Blank. Blank.
Blank. Blank. Blank. Blank.
Blank. Blank. Blank. Blank.
Blank. Blank. Blank. Blank.
Blank. Blank. Blank. Blank.
Blank. Blank. Blank. Blank.
Blank. Blank. Blank. Blank.
Blank. Blank. Blank. Blank.

"The Mute Gangster" was utterly crushed, on the verge of throwing in the towel.

The field of blank pages stretched on and on, no matter how far he went.

"The Mute Gangster" collapsed wearily in the middle of the field.

"Hang in there! Don't stop now!" I shouted.

"You're a gangster, remember! You can do it!" cried "The Short Gangster."

"Go on, don't give up!" yelled "The Fat Gangster."

"We'll always be together!" said "The Beautiful Gangster."

His unconquerable fighting spirit rekindled, "The Mute Gangster" trudged on.

4.

A very long time passed.

We spent the whole time in a state of extreme tension.

Finally, his voice wild and gravelly, "The Mute Gangster" bellowed out the words "Marbled chocolate!" "The Fat Gangster" and "The Beautiful Gangster" clasped hands and shook vigorously. "The Short Gangster" cried "Bravo!" and snapped his fingers.

"Marbled chocolate!" yelled "The Mute Gangster" again, as if to confirm that he had actually said it in the first place, pronouncing each syllable with tender, loving care. His utterance had the strength and the freshness of all originary speech.

"Go on," I said.

"Cracker-jacks, a treat in every box!" said "The Mute Gangster" without hesitation.

"Marbles."

"Tiddlywinks."

"Bully."

"Physical examination."

"Roundworm."

"Hernia."

"Crybaby."

"Blockhead."

"Bandylegged bozo."

"Dunce."

"Simpleton."

"Flatnosed fool."

"Ozaena."

"Yokel."

"Pervert."

"Premature ejaculation."

"Worthless gump."

"Opportunism."

"Thank you, that will be fine," I said.

"The Mute Gangster" continued talking, his face just as stiff as it had been before.

I put my arm around his shoulder and eased him down into his chair.

Then I turned to "The Fat Gangster."

"Okay, now it's your turn."

5.

"The Fat Gangster" stood up, still licking his lollipop.
He was just like his description on the Most Wanted
poster.

Name:	"The Fat Gangster"
Weight:	Extremely heavy
Personality:	Soft-spoken but very cruel
Characteristics:	Abnormally fond of lollipops
Hobbies:	Meditation
Favorite Author:	Edgar Rice Burroughs
Favorite Singer:	Marianne Faithfull
Favorite Words:	"We must love each other
	Lest we should die"
	—W.H. Auden

"I take it I'm allowed to choose my own theme?" said
"The Fat Gangster."
"Yes," I replied.
"Is it okay if I talk about candy?"
"Go right ahead."
From his breast pocket, "The Fat Gangster" removed a
handkerchief and spread it out on his desk, then set down on
it the lollipop he had been licking.
"I'm just crazy about cinnamon candy," said "The Fat
Gangster."
His voice was deep and rich and creamy. It had a really
thrilling ring.

"Peppermint candy is my second favorite. Cinnamon candies taste like angels, whereas peppermint candies taste like satyrs. These flavors are akin to one another in their hint of adventure, the kind Rilke sang of:

... *nur daß wir,*
mehr noch als Pflanze oder Tier
mit diesen Wagnis gehn, es wollen ...
(... Though, at least,
more daringly than plant or beast,
we will this daring, walk with it, and woo it ...)

Coconut candy is my third favorite. Its flavor has two utterly different aspects to it, like the expression on Botticelli's Venus. In the shadowy left-hand side of her face the artist presents us with an image of despair and of the languishing spirit; while in the illuminated right half he offers a vision of a spirit gazing loftily upwards, filled with strength and self-confidence. It is this somewhat bitter duality, one that prizes the synthesis of conflicting elements over simple unity, that one detects in the flavor of coconut candy."

"The Fat Gangster" fell silent, a bewildered look on his face.

I didn't know what to say either.

"The Beautiful Gangster" and "The Short Gangster" were stumped, too.

Only "The Mute Gangster," utterly insensible to the goings-on of the world, continued plodding onward through his empty field.

"I was only trying to talk about candy. I really didn't mean to *show off.*"

"Of course, I understand."

"I wanted to be accurate in what I was saying," said "The Fat Gangster."

He seemed rather crestfallen.

"It doesn't do any good to try and get it all out at once. Perhaps you ought to try telling us about these things while you're licking your lollipop. Will that help?"

"Is it okay for me to do that?"

"Sure, why don't you give it a try?"

"The Fat Gangster" took the lollipop from the handkerchief and popped it back into his mouth, then turned and gave me a smile.

Once again "The Fat Gangster" began talking, choosing his words as carefully as Roger Caillois.

6.

"We chose to become gangsters of our own free will.

We were neither obliged nor forced to do so.

If we should ever be presented with another chance to make the choice, I'm sure we would choose this life again, and choose it with pleasure."

7.

"We never considered ourselves to be specially entitled as gangsters, nor has our profession ever caused us to feel inferior."

8.

"It seemed to us that gangsterism was a relative concept. We believed that we were gangsters only in relation to the world, and that nothing but a change in that relationship could ever transform us into anything other than gangsters."

9.

"We adopted forms and styles that are generally understood to be *gangsterly*.

We tried not to behave in a fashion that would prove confusing; we did not indulge in unusual rhetoric. We did not attempt to become unique new gangsters.

Despite our best efforts, our behavior was sometimes perceived as 'deviant' or 'peculiar.' We refused, however, to make unwonted changes in our way of life simply for the sake of avoiding misunderstandings."

10.

"We never asserted that killing people and stealing money were means to creative or constructive ends. We're only gangsters, after all, not prophets."

11.

"We never claimed to possess a superior understanding of the world.

We did not claim JUSTICE, in any sense of the word, as the basis of our acts.

It seemed to us that insofar as our point of view was, like any other, a point of view, it had inevitable limitations; at the same time, we vowed not to have our hands tied by this knowledge.

If our point of view was nothing more than a link in an infinite chain of relativity, it seemed wiser to welcome this given of our existence than to rail at it."

12.

"We did not let it go to our heads, nor did we fret, when imitators began to appear; we felt no need to lecture them.

It seemed to us that they would discover soon enough just what the consequences of imitating us were."

13.

"In a sense, our stance on the money problem was pessimistic.

Because in this world, money is essentially *Schein*, which is to say, appearance.

Just as our existence is relative, money is relative.

The total sum of the moneys we make off with never exceeds the deduction limits specified before the event in the 'Casualty and Theft Losses' section of the tax code. In other words, considered mathematically, it's precisely as though we weren't committing robbery at all.

'Robbery' is nothing more than another program (or information) in an input-output analysis. 'Robbery' is nothing more than a *Schein* within *Schein*."

14.

"It's true that we sometimes pursued irrational dreams, but it never seemed to us that dreaming was something to be avoided.

In fact, it seemed an indispensable attribute of gangsterism.

We never intended to be *distilled water.*"

15.

"Things we believed had been proven beyond any doubt were frequently not seen in that light by others; at the same time, what others believed had been proven beyond doubt often appeared in a different light to us. Disagreements of this sort were constant.

It seemed to us that such a state of affairs should be welcomed with open arms. We tended to prefer viewpoints opposed to our own to those that lent us support."

16.

"We never tried to derive abstract ideas from our actions. Attempts of that nature always evoked in us a certain feeling of alarm, as did the contrary, those attempts to base actions on ideas.

We tried to derive our actions directly from common wisdom, from that wisdom that is so thoroughly universal that it is gradually coming to be forgotten."

17.

"Always after we carry out some deed, sitting at our desks at night, we feel such pangs of unease that it makes us dizzy. This is because we fear that every day, little by little, we are drifting away from the world.

We fear that in the end, everything we have accomplished has assumed a form exactly opposite to what we envisioned.

But on such nights, when our hearts and minds scream out with the desire to run from it all, to give up thinking altogether, we command ourselves to confront our fears.

You can't wield a machine gun if you've got your hands clapped over your eyes. You would cease to be a gangster."

18.

"The Fat Gangster" had finished speaking.

Nothing remained of his candy.

"The Fat Gangster" took another lollipop from his pocket.

"I'm not a very good speaker," said "The Fat Gangster."

"I meant to say something very different," he continued, "but somehow I'm not able to say it very well. When you've been a gangster for as long as I have, you start to lose the knack for this kind of thing."

19.

I turned to "The Beautiful Gangster."

"All right, it's your turn now. Go ahead."

"The Beautiful Gangster" rose to his feet.

"The Beautiful Gangster" gazed straight into Song Book's eyes.

"Come back," he said.

20.

"Come back."

"No."

"Come back."

"No. I'm not a gangster."

"You *are* a gangster."

"I'm *not* a gangster."

Song Book covered her face with her hands.

"Listen, babe, you're a gangster."

"No! No! No! I'm *sick* of being a gangster!"

"The Beautiful Gangster" aimed his pistol at Song Book's chest.

"I'm *SICK* of it!!"

"Don't!" I screamed. "Don't shoot!"

"The Fat Gangster," inhumanly strong, had me pinioned.

"The Beautiful Gangster" 's pistol spat a burst of flame.

I gazed at the red stain spreading across Song Book's white blouse.

Still covering her face, Song Book collapsed.

21.

The gangsters and I stood around Song Book's corpse.

Song Book's face was brown, and her lips were slightly ajar.

"Keep watching," said "The Fat Gangster," who still had me pinioned.

22.

I kept standing there.
"Henry IV" rubbed his nose against Song Book's body.
"Meeee, meeee," cried "Henry IV."

23.

Song Book's eyelids fluttered.

Gradually the color returned to her face.

"The Fat Gangster" was the first to speak.

"Gangsters don't die," he said.

"No matter how many times you take us down, we always come back to life," he said. "We can be killed and killed and killed, again and again—we come back to life every time. As long as our faces remain intact, we'll be gangsters forever, forever and ever."

24.

Song Book's eyes opened just a crack.

She didn't seem to have any idea where she was.

Song Book gazed at the gangsters and then me with glass eyes.

"The Fat Gangster" released me.

I knelt down by my prostrate lover and brushed the hair from her face.

"I'm so sorry."

Tears spilled from Song Book's glass eyes.

25.

"Song Book . . . please," I said. "What does 'Sayonara, Gangsters' mean?"

Someone brought the butt of a pistol down on my head, hard.

Everything around me was plunged in darkness.

II Very nice, very nice, very nice

1.

"Henry IV" and I sat goggling at the television screen.

2.

"All right, gangsters.
We have you completely surrounded.
Resistance is futile. Come out of there immediately.
Anyone who resists will be shot."

The blare of the armored police van's speakers bounced off the wall of the building where the gangsters had holed up and slowly disappeared into the dome of the sky.

3.

The entire building was cloaked in a fog of white, brown, and black smoke.

"The Fat Gangster" made his appearance, two swooning police officers tucked under his right arm. His body was riddled with holes. His left arm was swinging back and forth, half out of its socket, only barely managing to stay stuck.

"The Fat Gangster" kept walking. He had lost more than half his blood, and the resultant languor of his movements was so extreme it was frightening.

The officers trained their rifles on "The Fat Gangster" 's face.

"All right, now, put 'em up!"

"My hands, you mean? Would just one do?" sighed "The Fat Gangster" wearily. "Which do you fancy? The one I can move or the one I can't?"

"The Fat Gangster" looked so tired he could hardly keep awake.

"I'm warning you! Get those hands up now! We won't hold back if you don't!"

"You're gonna shoot even if I don't put 'em up, you mean? Why don't you just talk straight?"

Two rifle shots pierced "The Fat Gangster" 's right shoulder and side.

"The Fat Gangster" 's face twisted with pain. He dropped the lollipop he'd been sucking and the two police officers he'd been carrying. Coming to as they hit the ground, the officers noticed the lollipop lying in front of them and reached out to seize it.

"Get away, that's mine!!"

"The Fat Gangster" scooped up the lollipop an instant before the officers were able to grab it. Just then, another burst of flame exploded from the rifles.

"The Fat Gangster" lifted his head. Everything below his nose had been blown away, leaving nothing but a squishy, pulpy mess like a bowl of bright red oatmeal.

"The Fat Gangster" just stood there plunged in thought, still clutching his lollipop. He no longer had a mouth and couldn't figure out where to put the candy.

"The Fat Gangster" wiped the dirt that had stuck to his lollipop—*ah, the candy he loved best in the world!*—on the hem of his jacket, then tucked the confection into his breast pocket. Emitting a terrible groan, he began plodding dully onward in the direction of the odious little wretches from the police force who had shot off his mouth.

"Aim above his nose! Get him there and it'll be the end! Ready! AIM! *FIRE!!*"

4.

Someone ran out of the entrance of the building as it vomited black smoke and was firing his machine gun blindly in all directions as he ran.

It was "The Mute Gangster."

"Social phobia!"

"Flatfoot!"

"Skirt-lifter!"

"Blowin' in the wind!"

"The Mute Gangster" made a break for it, still shouting. But before he could run ten yards both his knees had been shot through, and he fell flat on his face.

"Some like it hot!"

"Kill him!"

"The Mute Gangster" was still sprawled there, preparing to return their fire with his machine gun, when the rain of bullets from the officers' machine guns, a single tremendous burst, pounded him. He sprang up and bounded around on the road, looking for all the world as if he were performing some new dance.

"The Mute Gangster" was hardly breathing now.

A policeman pried open his mouth and shoved in the barrel of a shotgun.

"Anything you wanna say?" said the policeman.

"I sure hope the weather will be nice tomorrow!"

"The Mute Gangster" bit down on the barrel.

"The Mute Gangster" 's face was wiped off the earth.

5.

"The Short Gangster" had lost all will to fight.

"The Short Gangster" had been hounded into the narrow crevice between an armored police van and one of the walls of the building. He lay there sobbing.

"Help me, help me, help me, help me!"

"I think not, buddy."

An abbreviated corps of three police officers rolled "The Short Gangster" over onto his back and held him down, fixing his head in place, whereupon a fourth policeman slung an enormous industrial-size hammer way up high over his head.

"Help me! Help me! Murderers!"

"Who's the murderer, asshole!"

"Sheesh, lately I just don't seem to be having much luck."

"The Short Gangster" sighed, then shut his eyes.

The hammer fell.

6.

They cut to a different scene.

Beside an armored car stood a policeman; he was eating his lunch.

A reporter was interviewing the policeman.

"So, how would you rate your performance today?"

"Oh, I'm doing okay, I guess."

"Must be tough, huh? Your life on the line and all?"

"Yeah, but that's my job, you know?"

"What do you think of the gangsters?"

"I don't really get it."

"What's in the lunchbox?"

"Fried shrimp, a hamburger and fish paste, boiled peas, a roll of fried egg, spinach with a soy-and-broth dressing, seven kinds of pickled veggies, and for desert, two tangerines."

"How do you like it? Is it good?"

"Yes."

"Well then, how about sending a little message out to your folks back in the country, on the far side of the screen?"

"Sure. Hey there, Dad! Hi Mom! It's me. I'm doing fine, working hard. I'll be back in August for the Festival of the Dead. Boy, that'll be fun, won't it?"

"Wave to them," said the reporter.

Still holding his chopsticks, the policeman waved his hand.

The reporter turned the mic in the direction of the next policeman in the line, who was also eating his lunch. The policeman turned away, hiding his tears.

"What's wrong? Has one of your buddies died?"

The policeman hurled his lunchbox at the television camera.

"Damn it, I hate fried shrimp!!!"

They cut to the TV studio.

"What's at the heart of these developments?" asked the newscaster.

"I have no idea," the expert on gangster issues replied.

"As I recall, there were five gangsters in all."

"Yes, yes, that's something I myself have pointed out in the past."

"What's more, one of them was a woman."

"Yes, yes, that's something I myself have pointed out in the past."

A saucy smile flickered at the corners of the newscaster's mouth.

"Ah, but what of the fact that the gangsters' only weakness lay in their faces? This news station was responsible for that discovery, wasn't it? Am I wrong?"

"And what of it?! Nobody's theory is perfect!! Where are your manners, bastard?!"

Grabbing the crowbar he had kept concealed underneath his chair, the expert on gangster issues sprang to his feet.

"No one disparages my research and gets away with it!"

Leaping to his feet, the newscaster whipped a pair of brass knuckles from his pocket, slipped one onto each fist, and made a few light jabs in the air.

"Interesting. Let's see if a senile old academic can down

me, huh?"

The gangster expert emitted a yowl and took a swing with his crowbar.

"Hi-yah! Argh, you little shit!"

Bringing a little sway-back action into play, the newscaster slipped clear of the flying crowbar and struck back with a staggering bodyslam. The gangster expert was gurgling, his body hunched, when the newscaster's fatal hook exploded against his right temple.

After confirming that the gangster expert was really dead, the newscaster flashed a peace sign at the television screen—two fingers raised in the shape of a V.

"Reality vs. Theory is over, folks! Reality wins! What a knockout!"

Then the building returned to the screen.

7.

A man and a woman were running across the roof of the building, holding hands.

It was Song Book and "The Beautiful Gangster." Song Book tugged "The Beautiful Gangster" along behind her as she ran. She had on a black silk dress that looked like some kind of underwear, her hair was permed, and she was very heavily made up. She was your typical gangster's mistress.

"The Beautiful Gangster" took a spill.

His eyes and ears were all wrapped up in bandages.

Song Book helped "The Beautiful Gangster" up, and they ran on.

Arriving at long last at the foot of an enormous water tower, Song Book and "The Beautiful Gangster" started up the ladder that led to the lookout platform all the way up at the tippy top.

8.

A strong wind was blowing over the lookout platform, making Song Book's hair and dress whip and flutter.

Song Book held down the hem of her dress with one hand.

Three helicopters bearing television cameras whipped and fluttered in the air over the heads of Song Book and "The Beautiful Gangster."

Removing a compact from her small handbag, Song Book redid her lipstick.

"The Beautiful Gangster" slumped motionless on the floor of the lookout platform, gazing up with unseeing eyes at Song Book fixing her makeup.

"All ready!" yelled Song Book, and placed a hand on "The Beautiful Gangster"'s shoulder.

After helping up "The Beautiful Gangster," Song Book led him to the very edge of the platform.

After unbuttoning "The Beautiful Gangster"'s shirt and exposing his chest, Song Book placed a knife in his hand.

"Where are they?" asked "The Beautiful Gangster."

"Over that way."

Song Book rotated "The Beautiful Gangster"'s body with both hands so that he faced the cluster of armored police vans.

"You're fine now."

"Okay."

Arms still outstretched, Song Book stepped backwards to the opposite edge of the platform.

"The Beautiful Gangster" plunged the knife into the left side of his chest and pulled it across to the right until he reached the middle, then yanked it down, slashing himself wide open. An absolutely unbelievable quantity of blood was now gushing from "The Beautiful Gangster"'s chest.

"The Beautiful Gangster" was struggling, trying to thrust his hand into the mouth of the wound. He couldn't see a thing, of course, and the knife he was using wasn't quite as sharp as he could have wished. After all the trouble he took, he hadn't been able to make a very clean cut.

"Mercy," said "The Beautiful Gangster" as he began slashing away once more, up and down and side to side and diagonally and this way and that way. If he didn't get this over with soon, he'd faint from losing too much blood.

Plunging the knife into his chest, "The Beautiful Gangster" attempted to slice out the thing he was looking for.

Swooning, "The Beautiful Gangster" gripped the upper half of his stomach, which he had managed to cut loose, and lifted it high over his head.

"This is my heart, right?" he asked Song Book.

"Yep," replied Song Book.

"The Beautiful Gangster" slung the upper half of his stomach at the armored police vans looking up at him.

"Sheesh! What a job that was!"

"The Beautiful Gangster" leaned on the railing, barely able to stand.

"Wait a second! There's still something beating in my

chest!"

"It's your lungs, they beat too! Don't you remember learning that in school?"

"Did we learn that? I guess I'd forgotten. Man, I'm pooped."

"The Beautiful Gangster" 's pallid face bowed down all of a sudden. Letting his knife fall on the platform, he shoved himself over the railing.

"This really sucks—couldn't be any worse."

"The Beautiful Gangster" plunged headfirst to the ground.

Bending to pick up the knife from where it lay in the sticky pool of blood shed by "The Beautiful Gangster," Song Book allowed the two straps of her dress to fall lightly away from her shoulders.

Song Book's breasts stiffened as they came in contact with the air.

Song Book jabbed the knife in under her left breast, and then, with it stuck there, she swung around to face the television screen and grimaced.

9.

"This sucks. Really."

10.

"It really sucks when it sucks."

11.

I turned off the television.

"That's enough, isn't it?" I said to "Henry IV."

"Meogh," whined "Henry IV" from his basket. "Meogh."

"I guess even gangsters die."

"Meogh."

"And now Song Book's dead, too."

"Meogh."

"I wonder what they'll do with the gangsters' bodies."

"Meogh."

"Do you think they'll have a proper funeral and all?"

"Meogh."

"Do you suppose City Hall sent death notices to the gangsters, too?"

"Meogh."

I stood up. "Henry IV" and I hadn't had a bite to eat during TV time.

"You want something to eat?" I asked.

"Canned tuna? Grilled mackerel?" I asked. "How about a milk-and-vodka?"

"Henry IV" kept his face buried in the old towel at the bottom of his basket.

"I don't feel like eating," he said. "I want to read Thomas Mann. Do you think maybe you could go buy a collection of his stories for me?"

"Sure thing."

And so I set out in search of some Thomas Mann.

12.

None of the bookstores had any collections of stories by Thomas Mann. The writer Thomas Mann had never existed in the first place. No doubt the sadness of it all had driven "Henry IV" mad. Song Book had been "Henry IV" 's mother, sister, lover, and comrade, and now that she was dead "Henry IV" had lost his marbles.

13.

I'd already gotten several refills on my whisky at the bar. I was pooped.

"Tell me, you ever hear of Thomas Mann?" I asked the bartender.

"Can't say that I have."

"He's a nonexistent writer. This cat I know got a bit screwy when his mistress died, and now he's saying he wants to read stories by this Thomas Mann character."

"I see. Sounds like he's quite a romantic cat."

"What, because he likes to read?"

"No, that's not what I mean. After all, my old cat used to read the paper. She'd go through the morning edition as soon as it came, before I could. The whole thing, from the editorials to the stock quotes. And then she would trot in and climb up on bed, right by my head, because I'd still be sleeping, and tell me the news.

'Hey, master, the political situation in the Middle East is unstable. I think it might be wise to stock up on Scotch whisky before the Suez Canal is blockaded,' she'd say. Or maybe, 'Interest rates have been lowered 0.5% and it looks like they may be lowered a further 0.5% before too long, so now's the time to sell your government bonds.'

But my cat never read novels. Conventional wisdom has it that people who read novels stop being able to make accurate judgments, you know."

"I've got to bring back a collection of stories by Thomas

Mann, I've simply got to! 'Henry IV' is at home waiting for me right now."

"Looks like you're in a nice little fix, huh?"

"What should I do? You think I can just tell him there's no such writer?"

"On a different note, how 'bout it, wanna see my back? I've got wings."

Turning away from me, the bartender began unzipping his back.

"Stop it! I don't wanna see! Get away from me!"

"Not even a little peek? Oh well. Too bad."

The bartender had unzipped himself about a third of the way. He started zipping himself back up, but it was hard because the zipper kept getting caught on his wings.

"I'm terribly sorry, but do you think you could give me a hand?"

In the end, I had to pull the bartender's zipper down as far as his bottom and tuck his wings back into place in order to zip him up.

"Would you stop moving your wings?"

"I'm sorry, but I can't help it. They move on their own."

"Man, these wings of yours sure do smell. You ever take a bath?"

"Sorry, I'd drown if I took a bath. Ah, that's better. Many thanks."

14.

I was getting dizzy.

"You're a gangster, aren't you?" said the woman.

"Mmm."

"I knew it as soon as you came in! Listen, how'd you like to do it with me? I've never done it with a gangster before, and I don't wanna grow old never having got it on with a gangster! Come on. I saw you've got a swell limp. Hey, are you listening to me?"

"Mmm. Have you got wings, too?"

"Oh, are you a poet? I don't mind if you're a poet. I do it with poets *all* the time, the first time I ever did it was when I was eleven, and the guy I did it with then was a poet, I've done it with so many poets that I am just sick to *death* of them. But the person I've done it with most is my brother, man oh man my brother was the greatest, wanna hear about my brother?"

"I take it you don't have wings, then?"

"My brother used to come and sit by my pillow every night. 'What's up, big brother?' 'I thought you might want to hear the story of Little Red Riding Hood.' 'What's up, big brother?' 'I had this dream, and in the dream you were dying.' 'What's up, big brother?' 'I'm just gonna stay here and watch over you, to make sure the monsters don't come in and eat you.'

Actually he just wanted to do it with me. 'Hey, big brother, you can come in under the covers if you want to.'

'No no no, that's not it, it's not because I want your body that I'm here.' So then my brother and I started doing it every night, but my brother was always telling me, 'No no no no no, it's not because I want your body'—I didn't get it at all.

But my brother was really good in bed, no one else can make me feel like that."

"I have to buy a collection of stories by Thomas Mann to take home."

"I mean, it's *okay* if you're a poet, I don't mind. It just always seemed to me like it would be really great to do it with a *gangster* sometime. I found poets interesting at first, you know, but they're all so bad at it, they really are, and they all handle my body with such *violence*, I just hate being handled *violently*, I like for people to be nice and gentle with me the way my brother always was.

Everything's been so awful since my brother died, you know, and I guess I'd been hoping maybe somewhere there was a gangster for me, one who'd treat me nice."

I raised my head. The woman had on a see-through black silk dress, over the top of which spilled two breasts, each one about as large as a baby's head. A bright red manicure, a bright red pedicure, bright red lips.

"This is the big thing now. Mistress style. Didn't you see her on TV?"

Taking up a spoon, the woman pretended to make a slash under her left breast.

" 'Wait a second! There's still something beating in my chest!'

'It's your lungs, they beat too! Don't you remember

learning that in school?'

'Did we learn that? I guess I'd forgotten. Man, I'm pooped.' "

Rolling back her eyes and drooling, the woman let her head plop onto the bar.

" 'This really sucks—couldn't be any worse.'

Hey, how was that? Did it look real?"

"Mmm."

"You want to do it with me?"

"Mmm."

"Well, c'mon then, let's go."

The woman rose to her feet. I found myself standing up with her.

"Over this way. I always do it in the toilet, you don't have to worry about people watching if you do it in the toilet."

Clad in nothing but his undies, the bartender was executing figure eights round and round the two chandeliers that hung from the ceiling of the bar.

"Ladies and gentlemen!" shouted the bartender.

He kept flying around, skimming the ceiling.

"These wings of mine are REAL!"

"Look, the bartender's flying," I said.

"Oh, he's just pretending to be a poet. Who cares. C'mon, let's go."

15.

When we got to the toilet, the woman began taking off everything she had on. It wasn't hard. All she had to do was remove her dress and her underwear and her girdle and her garters and her stockings, and she was naked.

"Go on, you take off yours, too. But only from the waist down, you can keep on your shirt and all. I'm not into any of that *perverse* stuff."

I took off my jeans and my underwear and hung them on the door.

"Hey."

"What?"

"You got a hanky on you?"

"Yeah."

"Can I borrow it? I tend to shout a lot, so I wanna stuff it in my mouth."

"Sure."

The woman rolled up the hanky and inserted it into her mouth.

"It seems like I'm raping you or something."

The woman took the hanky out from her mouth, then slapped my cheek, hard.

"I *hate* that word!"

"I take it back."

The woman swallowed the hanky once more, then placed her hands and her head against the wall, swiveling her large white bottom my way.

I actually had an erection. I could hardly believe it.

The woman looked back over her shoulder. Once again she removed the hanky.

"Hey."

"What is it this time?"

"If we do it like this, I can't even tell that I'm doing it with a gangster."

"That's true."

"If I'm doing it with a gangster, I want to see the gangster."

"Well, why don't you turn around to face me?"

"Oh, how *monstrous*! Didn't I tell you I'm not into *perverse* stuff?!"

The woman applied the hanky, now all gummed-up with her spit, to her eyes.

The woman began sobbing.

"No one *ever* does it with me, never, I know it's because I have my likes and dislikes, I'm particular, and I don't *want* to do it with any more poets, I just *don't*, and here I've finally managed to find you, and you're a gangster, but you won't even do it with me."

"I think I can manage it," I told the woman.

"Really? You *can*?" said the woman.

The woman's eyes were moist with tears. It struck me that her face had a certain remarkably innocent look to it.

Until then I hadn't really taken a good look at her face.

"Are you in high school?"

"I should think *not*! I'm in junior high. How do you wanna do it?"

"Okay, how's this. I'll run around by the sink, dragging my foot, and you can get it on by yourself while you watch me. How do you like that?"

"Oh, yes! I love that, let's do that!"

I opened the door to our toilet stall.

I ran around and around in front of the sink, dragging my leg on the tiled floor.

The young woman leaned against the door of the stall and gazed at me.

She poured everything she had into her onanistic pleasures.

"Keep *running*! Keep *running*!"

Around and around and around and around I ran, as fast as I could manage.

My feet slipped on the wet tiles and I crashed. A bloody knee. Pain.

"Liar! You said you'd run for me! Don't stop *now*!"

I kept running around in front of the sink, my weenie swinging.

I was dizzy. I was dizzy. Man, was I dizzy.

16.

The young woman had a big, long orgasm.
An orgasm like a baby, like a flower.

17.

"Are you okay?" I asked the young woman.

The young woman lay stretched out on the floor of the toilet stall.

"It's so cold," murmured the young woman, in a tiny voice. She just lay there limply, like a doll, as I put her panties and dress back on her. This was a lot more trouble than getting them off had been. And with her lying there in a state like that, it didn't really make much difference whether she had them on or not.

"Sorry? Did you say something?" I said.

18.

"Listen, are you a gangster or a poet?"

19.

I lifted up the young woman and carried her out of the bathroom.

The young woman was sleeping like a baby.

"Big brother, big brother," murmured the young woman in her sleep.

Back in the bar, I laid the young woman down on a row of seats.

The customers were all flying around in the air, glasses in hand.

"Big brother, big brother."

Some drunk bozo who was up there clinging to the chandelier and flap-flapping his wings yowled, "Nevermore!"

20.

"How much?" I asked the bartender.

The bartender had his elbows propped on the bar. He was tearing at his hair.

"Oh god! Today is the worst day of my entire life!

Just look at this! I have webbed hands!"

The bartender's hands were webbed. You couldn't really tell when he had them closed, but it was plain as day when he opened them.

"Look, I'm leaving. How much do I owe you?"

"I wasn't hiding them. I hadn't even noticed them! Please believe me!"

"I believe you."

21.

"Shall I tell you about my wife?"

"Maybe next time."

"You'll find it a very interesting story. I've never told any-one."

"I've got a cat waiting for me at home. He's waiting for me to bring him some Thomas Mann. I've got to go buy it for him. I'm going."

I stepped away from the bar counter.

22.

Some drunk guy had come down and was leaning on the back of one of the chairs where the young woman was sleeping.

The drunk guy gazed down at the young woman.

Two little wings were starting to grow on the young woman's back.

"Big brother, big brother."

The drunk guy flew back up into the air.

23.

I could make myself Thomas Mann's *deputy*. It was so simple, why on earth hadn't I thought of it before? I'm telling you, my mind is definitely going.

All I had to do was bring a different book, put a cover over it and then go in and say, "Here you are, 'Henry IV', take a look. I've brought you Thomas Mann, like you asked me to." I'd open the book. "Hmmm, now let's see here, which of these shall we read first. . ." Only, this part would take some thought. Just what sort of stories should I put in the book? I couldn't let "Henry IV" get suspicious. These couple of days were crucial. A couple of days and "Henry IV" was bound to snap out of it. Absolutely. One day he might ask me, "By the way, I've been wondering about that Thomas Mann stuff you read me the other day. I may be wrong, but I have a feeling there's actually no such author. . ." But when that happens, I could just apologize. "I'm sorry, 'Henry IV'. You were so eager to read Thomas Mann that I made him up for you myself." And he'd say, "No kidding? Wow. Those stories weren't bad, you know."

Well then, I have to throw together a tale or two—stories that seem to go with the name Thomas Mann. And I have to do it fast. I need a *title* first, whatever, anything'll do. "John Lennon vs. The Martians"—no, no, that's a bit too much isn't it, you certainly wouldn't call that a Thomas Mannish title, no, no, it'll have to be something different, how about "Man's Fate?"—nah, that's no good either, Thomas Mann wouldn't be so inelegant, it's gotta be something finer and more *ironisch*—gravity, something with the word gravity, something with weight and a bit of color, how about this one, "Gravity and Repulsion," no no no, that's no title for a work of literature, "The Love of Gravity," that's not literary enough either, "The Butcher and Gravity," oh man that's *good*! That's it, "The Butcher and Gravity," and it can begin "The first one to notice was the butcher," that day all his customers left with puzzled looks on their faces, the one who bought the liver, the one who bought the prime sirloin, the one who bought the pork ribs, and the one who bought the drumsticks, every one of them went out with a puzzled look on his or her face, it happened when they looked at the scales, and the old lady who'd come for chicken skin at twenty yen per hundred grams presented the butcher with a little query—"Is today a sale day or something? You're giving me ten grams extra"— but you see the butcher had been butchering and nothing but for a good fifty-one years now, the man didn't even have to look at the scales, he was never off, not even by as little as a gram, and so—"That's odd"—he kept weighing the skins over and over, but every time they drifted over, and so the butcher pulled down the shutter that covered his storefront at night and put up a sign—"As of today this store will be closed. Thank you for many years of devoted patronage. –The Owner"—and after washing himself very well in the shower he rubbed his entire body with salt, garlic, and black sesame seeds, spreading it all perfectly evenly, he stuffed first his foot and then the rest of him into the thundering, moaning meat mincer—"My days are over. Adieu, Matsuzaka Beef, old friend. Goodbye, muscle-bound cows of Australia. *Da svidaniya*, dear frankfurter sausages!"—and in the midst of his misunderstanding the butcher went to his death, he died, though it was not the butcher who was mistaken but rather gravity, it just so happened that on that particular day gravity was just a little bit stronger than usual . . . no no no no, this is awful, this isn't a story at all, the title's to blame, I should just make gravity the theme of the piece, yes, that's it—"The Day When It Simply Wasn't Possible to Fly"—that's better now, much more staid—"The birds fell from the sky. Sparrows, bush warblers, even Jonathan Livingston Seagull was grounded"—people crawled abjectly along the ground when they wanted to walk, and elephants and hippopotamuses and trade centers collapsed, unable to bear their own weight, and a rocket launched at Cape Kennedy only made it 30 centimeters off the ground before it suddenly switched into reverse and dropped with a bang on its bottom and then just sat there on the ground, the whole situation was tragic, really tragic, and yet even as the entire world was raising cries of agony under the weight of the iron chains of gravity that bound it, there was a certain band of people who had the gall to go about in a state of perfect ecstasy: these were the members of "The Anti-Aeroplaneism Society"—"With the exception of birds, nothing heavier than air could possibly succeed in flying through the skies. After all, our Creator has unveiled no new works since the fifth day of creation!"—the members of this group denied that the Wright Brothers had ever flown—"Houdini achieved far more stunning magical effects!"—and denied as well, in a single all-encompassing sweep, the existence of Lindbergh's dual-propeller plane, the zero fighters launched from Japanese aircraft carriers during WWII, Tsiolkovskian helicopters, artificial satellites, intercontinental missiles, and live television broadcasts from Jupiter—"Come on, no one but children and *communists* would ever fall for a trick as obvious as that!"—in this manner did "The Anti-Aeroplaneism Society" waltz into its day of glory, and all the world was spring—"Yeah, what'd we tell you, huh? Oh, we warned you, we told you this whole aeroplane business was nothing but a pack of lies, 'cause there was no way any of those contraptions could ever fly, no way! Ha ha ha, serves you right, suckers!"—and every day the members of "The Anti-Aeroplaneism Society" would lie on their stomachs in the Society's office, flapping their hands and feet, slithering forward and making left turns and so on just like alligators, they constantly got together for drinks, and once the members of "The Anti-Aeroplaneism Society" were drunk and feeling good about themselves they would wriggle up the stairs, hooting and cawing and generally making one hell of a racket and cluster around the second floor window to heap scorn on all those "children" and "communists" crawling abjectly over the surface of the earth, for all creatures living were plastered to the face of the earth, slinking and inching and wriggling and scooting exhaustedly forward, and things that just couldn't wiggle and things that were awkwardly shaped and things that had been designed according to the principle of the golden mean were mercilessly and without exception crushed and smushed and crumpled and torn, yes, the office supervisor was the first to start bellowing down at them all, supporting his chin with both hands so that gravity wouldn't cause it to drop off—"Blea-a-a-a-a! If ya don't like it down there whyn't ya get up and fly? Hsst, ya dumbasses! Thought y'could fly!!"—"Hey, there! Let's see some flying, huh? Have you no shame?"—"Hey, guys, what happened to your planes?! Where'd all those fine jets of yours run off to now? Ha ha ha ha, take that, you underbrained louts!"—and goodness gracious, how annoyingly loud they were, these ridiculous yahoos shouting and hollering at the top of their lungs, and the fools just kept right at it until finally the ledge of the window snapped, and the whole lot of them plunged toward the ground, and then a "communist" who was crawling abjectly along, emitting moans and groans with every wiggle, heading to the supermarket behind his building to buy a package of Cup o' Noodles, this "communist" heard strange voices overhead, and looking up he realized that it was the members of "The Anti-Aeroplaneism Society" flailing their arms and legs about, tossing down a barrage of curses as they slowly climbed into the sky—"Hah, serves yah right!!! Now the whole damn earth has dropped!!!"—and the members of the society kept on rising and rising up and up until they found themselves in the bosom of the Creator, and then.

24.

I was crouched down on the road, retching, when the shining form seized me by the scruff of my neck.

"Who are you?" barked the shining form. "What are you doing here?"

The shining form was a police officer. He had attached flashlights all over his body and had them all turned on—that's why he'd appeared to me as a shining form. The officer kept the two flashlights on his helmet and the two in his hands trained directly on my face.

"Who are you? What are you doing here?"

"I can't find my house, I've lost my way."

Flashlights jutted out from the officer's chest and shoulders, and there were numerous others tucked in under the entire length of his belt, facing alternately up and down, and his combat boots were entirely covered with midget bulbs that winked on and off like neon signs.

"Who are you? Show me your ID card!"

I got my ID card out of my back pocket and attempted to pass it over to the shining policeman.

"Who told you to do that, you ass! Trying to kill me or something?"

The shining policeman delivered an explosive head-butt to the bridge of my nose, and I flopped back on the road, face up.

Evidently the policeman had gotten somewhat excited. There was a dull drone like the sound of an electric generator, and the flashlights enveloping the policeman's body began blinking rapidly on and off.

"Hang in there, bud!" said the policeman gently. "Are you okay?"

"Yeah, I'm okay."

The policeman put an arm around my shoulder and helped me sit up.

"Your nose is bleeding. Here, use this."

The policeman passed me a tissue.

"I bet you're wondering why I'm lit up like this, huh?"

"Yes."

"I'm scared of dark places. So I provide the light. Let me tell you, it was hard as hell getting myself ready to do it. But I wanted to live. You think I was right?"

"Yes."

"I think I was right, too. And of course I look cool, too. You got that ID?"

"Yes."

The shining policeman examined my ID, illuminating it from a variety of angles.

"I don't get this. I have no idea what you are," said the policeman. "And what's more, the question of what you are really doesn't concern me, does it?"

After looking over all the flashlights attached to his body and confirming that they were in proper working order, the policeman shone with all his strength.

"Ah, now that's bright! Wow, is that bright! Gosh, do I look awesome!"

Shrouded in blinding white light, the policeman walked away.

"Man, am I bright! Oh, don't I look splendid shining all white! Brighter, brighter!! Now, let's *really* shine!"

25.

"Henry IV" was sitting in his basket, way back in the back of the room.

His body had shrunk to half its former size.

"Hey, 'Henry IV,' I totally forgot that we have a collection of stories by Thomas Mann right here on the book shelf. I should've stopped to think about it. You want me to read it to you right now?"

"Henry IV" shook his head.

Even as I watched, "Henry IV" gradually continued to shrink.

"Hey, wouldn't you like a little something to eat? How about a beer? Come on, don't you at least want some milk?"

"Henry IV" shook his head.

"Henry IV" had shrunk to a fourth of his former size.

He just lay there in his basket, gazing up at the ceiling, not even blinking.

"How about the newspaper? I bet there'll be some interesting articles!"

"Okay," replied "Henry IV" in a voice like a cricket's.

I put my hand into the mailbox.

Inside I found the morning edition, and a postcard.

A black-bordered postcard from City Hall.

26.

"Henry IV," I said, "you're going to die tonight."

27.

Little by little, "Henry IV" was dying.

Death began in the lower half of "Henry IV"'s body.

First he stopped being able to move his legs and his tail.

By the time his sphincter died and slackened and he stopped being able to control his excretions, the tip of his tail had turned black and was starting to rot.

28.

"Henry IV" was in pain.

His respiratory organs were starting to go. Every time a convulsion ran through his throat or his bronchial tubes or some muscle in his chest, "Henry IV" 's still living upper half would writhe violently, struggling to take in air.

The night was still young.

"Henry IV" had much, much more writhing to do before he died.

29.

"Henry IV" was now no bigger than a twenty-day-old mouse.

"Hey," said "Henry IV."
"Are you in pain? Is there anything I can do for you?"
"I feel a little better now. How much longer do I have to go through this?"
"Oh, another three hours or so, I'd guess," I said. In truth it was another six.
"There's something I want you to do for me," said "Henry IV." His body gave off a really terrible odor. The odor kept drifting up to my nose. "Just kill me now."
"Oh, no. I can't do that."
"I'm not asking you to kill me because I'm in pain. It's because this is humiliating. I can't stand this smell. I don't want to smell even worse than this as I die."
"No, no. You saw the postcard, right? Hang in there just a little longer."

When he was seized by his next convulsion, "Henry IV" shredded his nose with his left forepaw, which he was still free to move.
"It stinks, it stinks. Why do I smell so awful?"
"Henry IV" was sobbing.

30.

I placed "Henry IV" on the palm of my hand.

"You sure have gotten small, haven't you?"

I felt around for "Henry IV" 's *medulla* with my index finger.

"Ah, that feels good," said "Henry IV."

I placed a pin up against "Henry IV" 's *medulla*.

"What does 'it really sucks' mean, anyway?" said "Henry IV."

I pushed the pin in.

31.

It was only on the sheets. And only when I used my right hand. This was the conclusion at which I arrived.

I noticed it last night. Strange. All these little critters appearing on my bed.

I would lie there with my hands splayed out on either side of me. Then after a while I would move my hands. And in the place where my right hand had been, the little critters would appear.

The same problem occurred with my bed cover, and with the bottom sheet. Also on the carpet covering the floor, and in the kitchen sink. Once, a critter appeared on a curtain, but it only happened once and it was defective, a little creature like a cross between an onion and a person. All I had to do was give the curtain a little shake, and it was gone.

The critters looked almost exactly like chicks that had had their wings plucked off. No sooner had they appeared on my sheets than they'd start pecking away at each other with their sharp beaks.

After hurling itself into the pleasures of a full hour of pecking, the one who had succeeded in eating all the rest would lie down with his bulging-to-bursting stomach sticking into the air, and die. Caught up in the excitement, it had overeaten.

I was staring down at my sheets.
A thrill ran through my chest. I was waiting for a new

critter to appear.

The first little critter appeared.

It was the spitting image of "The Fat Gangster."

Licking away at his lollipop, he put his feet up on the "The Mute Gangster" 's newly arrived head.

"You've got to work on your vocabulary," said "The Fat Gangster."

"The Fat Gangster" was now standing up very straight. Right behind him, the hat of "The Beautiful Gangster" and "The Short Gangster" 's machine gun were in the process of entering the world.

32.

I heard a voice.

"I wish I knew whether it was morning or night now. If it were morning, I'd get up and take a walk, but if it were night I'd go to sleep."

Thinking it over, I realized the voice was mine.

33.

I was counting the critters.

One. Two. Three. Four. Five. Six. Seven. Eight. Nine. Ten.

"Eleven."

"Twelve."

"Thirteen."

"Fourteen."

The critters started stating their own numbers before I could.

"Fifteen."

"Sixteen."

34.

I have a bad feeling about this.

35.

A very bad feeling.

36.

I've had a bad feeling about things ever since I was born. How on earth could I have forgotten? And yet . . .
I'm starting to remember.
You know, my voice has just gotten so hoarse. So hoarse it's sad.
I hate voices like this. I like . . . I like . . . I like . . .
A very different kind of voice.

37.

I've started feeling . . . a little bit nice.
Yes, indeed.
I have a very nice, very nice, very nice feeling.

38.

See there? Even my voice is getting younger.
Little by little.

39.

I took the basket containing "Henry IV" 's corpse and went up to the river that flows on the sixth floor.

The sixth floor was windier that day than I had ever seen it.

Almost all the light had been blown away, making it as dark as night.

I set the basket on the surface of the river.

The wind was so strong that the water near the banks of the river was flowing in the wrong direction, back toward the source. After heading up the river for a while, the basket finally moved in closer to the middle of the river, and began drifting back down in the right direction, downstream.

40.

Something was flying in the sky, but it was too dark for me to make it out.

Then, in between two winds, a tangle of dozens of streams of light, all long and thin, like search lights, illuminated a young woman flying in the sky.

Two brilliantly white wings, each much longer than the young woman was tall, trailed out behind her back. I couldn't imagine what made the young woman want to go out flying on a day when the wind was so terribly strong.

The young woman wasn't very skilled with her wings, and the wind was buffeting her about, playing with her. The young woman would pirouette down all of a sudden until she skimmed the surface of the water, then rocket up 100 yards into the air.

"Big brother, big brother."

The young woman was sucked into a pocket of turbulence that tore off one of her wings and sent it zooming away.

The young woman tumbled into the river, somewhere far downstream.

41.

I went shopping in the supermarket.

Five black suits. Borsolino hats. I stared into the eyes of the gangster expert's *Encyclopedia of Gangster Habiliments* and it stared into mine, and we waited to see who would be the first to laugh. This was how I chose my clothes.

Machine guns. Pistols. Bullet clips. Knives. Also a selection of lollipops. Cinnamon, peppermint, coconut.

The girl at the register flashed me a smile so amiable I thought she might hug me.

"Are you going to play gangsters, sir?"

"I'm going to be a gangster."

"Oh my!"

"Don't bother punching these things in. I'm going to steal them."

"Oh my oh my!"

You use Wella shampoo, I can tell. You smell just like Song Book.

I grabbed a machine gun from my shopping cart and aimed it five inches over the girl's head. She was completely absorbed in the task of punching in my purchases.

"Excuse me, would you mind covering you ears? This will be very loud."

"Oh my!"

The girl ceased her punching and gleefully covered her ears. Such service.

"Is this all right?"

"Yes, fine. Domo arigato."

I blasted away.

42.

I was wandering restlessly this way and that through the museum, a machine gun slung over my shoulder.

"You got some business with me?" said an old man in bronze from his pedestal.

"No, I do not have any business with you," I replied.

"No business with me? None at all? No interest in me?"

"I'm looking for a different old man, not you."

"I'm an old man. Won't I do?"

"Look, I don't have time to bother with you. I'm in a hurry."

"Oh, I see. I get it. You're a lousy, rotten, blockheaded, super-duper dunce, that's the problem. Go on, get the hell out of here, you dumbass!"

Blushing brightly with embarrassment, I fled the old man in bronze.

43.

I stopped before a statue that looked as if it probably depicted "The Gangster Expert Beaten to Death by the Newscaster."

"Hey, let me see your face."

"No, you can't."

"Because you're so ugly, is that it?"

"It's no good. Bait me all you like, I won't fall for it."

"You know what I am?"

"You appear to be dressed as a gangster. Hmph. Just your style, I suppose?"

"I've come here to kill you."

All of a sudden the sculpture of "The Gangster Expert" chucked a handful of sand at my eyes. Then, while I ducked, he leapt down from his pedestal and ran.

I glanced around the gallery.

I discovered the back of the statue of "The Gangster Expert" amidst a cluster of figures carved in relief on a column over in a corner of the room. The statue had shoved its way in, even though there really wasn't enough space.

"You're nabbed."

I tapped the shoulder of the statue of "The Gangster Expert," which had crept down in between the skirts of Andromeda and Athena, both part of the relief. The statue was weeping quietly.

"Oh, what a mess I am. Oh, please don't laugh at me. As soon as I started thinking I was going to be killed, my body just moved on its own. See, I once had to go through the experience of being killed—you know that, right? It's really scary, let me tell you. It's happened to me once, and once is enough. Why do you want to kill me?"

"I don't really know."

"Man, try having someone come and kill *you* without knowing why. Okay, then, okay, hurry up and kill me. Forget the machine gun, I can't stand noise. You've got a knife on you, I presume?"

I took out the knife and prepared myself.

"Hey! What the hell's up with you? You're shaking!"

"I've never killed anyone before."

"Sheesh! Listen, put the palm of your hand up against the butt of the knife and then when you come at me throw the weight of your body against it. You don't stab me, you bump into me, got that? Okay? You ready? All right, come on!"

44.

The knife slid into the body of the statue of "The Gangster Expert" as easily as if it were made of butter.

"It's a hit! Oh, that was wonderful—oh, oh that was crappy!"

The statue of "The Gangster Expert" collapsed jelly-like into my arms.

"God it hurts. Oh god does it hurt, getting killed like this. Hey, how does it feel now that you've finally gone and committed murder? What the hell, you're crying? Come on, don't get all sentimental on me now."

I gazed into the eyes of the statue of "The Gangster Expert."

"Sorry, bud, but we statues don't have pupils. If you've finished your work here why don't you just skedaddle, huh? I'm gonna die in one hell of an awful state in a little while, you realize. Don't embarrass me any more than you already have."

I laid the statue of "The Gangster Expert" out on its original pedestal.

It felt like a deflated rubber doll.

When I fled from the gallery, holding my head in my hands, the statue of "The Gangster Expert" was clutching the knife I'd stabbed it with. It sang very quietly.

"It hurts
it hurts
it hurts

and
I'm afraid
I'm afraid
I'm afraid
killed twice
and what's more
not a hint of tragedy either time
and so   no one will remember me
how sad
how sad
is my death."

45.

The young woman at the front desk of "The Children's Graveyard" followed me around like my shadow, gazing admiringly at the movements of my hands as I meandered here and there, setting up the time bombs.

"Hey."

"What is it?"

"Why do you put concrete blocks around the bombs? It seems like a lot of trouble."

"The explosion has to occur within a closed-off space if you want there to be a blast of any great magnitude. Listen here, these bombs are going to go off in another ten minutes. If I were you I'd stop chatting with me and make a run for it."

With an elegant gesture, the young woman consulted her Mickey Mouse watch.

"I'd like to, but unfortunately I'm still on duty. I just can't get away."

"Oh well, too bad. In that case, it's important that you try and get to a place with the thickest walls possible, avoiding anything made of glass, and then maybe crawl under a desk or something. I don't know, maybe then it won't be so bad."

"I'll give that a try. Well, see you around."

"Sorry to put you to so much trouble."

"Yeah, it is kind of a pain. A strange thing for you to say, though, isn't it?"

Still smiling broadly, the young woman headed back to the front desk.

I suppose it was sort of a strange thing for me to say.

46.

Three seconds.
Two seconds.
I put my thumb in my mouth and started sucking.

47.

I walked back inside "The Children's Graveyard," feeling totally crushed. There had been no bang. There was no flash, no burst of wind. Everything was just as it had been. Inside the graveyard, the endless tape of the famous elegy trilled on peacefully, just as before.

48.

The young woman at the front desk was lying on the floor.

There was a huge hole in her side, so huge a child could have crawled inside.

"Hey, wake up! Wake up!"

Kneeling down, I gave the cheeks of the shut-eyed young woman a succession of slaps. Her eyes opened half way, but only half way.

"Hey, what happened?" I asked.

"Man, that was amazing! My whole body just went numb. It was like my womb had been blown out or something."

The young girl frowned. Her face was deathly pale.

"It's weird, it feels sort of like I've got a hole in my stomach."

"Just your imagination."

"Yeah. I'm something of a hypochondriac."

The young woman closed her eyes.

She'll probably never open her eyes again, I thought.

The young woman opened her eyes again.

"It's funny, I feel like I'm dying."

"Just your imagination."

"Yeah, I know."

The young woman closed her eyes. It was the end. This time she really did die, one-hundred percent, all the way.

Suddenly the woman leapt to her feet and started walking away.

"Hey, hey, what's up? Where are you going?"

"My handbag! I left my handbag in the drawer! Oh, oh, where's my desk?"

The young woman was sobbing. She couldn't see anymore.

"It's okay, don't worry! Don't worry! I'll go get it for you. You just lie there, okay? Okay? I'll run get it for you. I'll be right back."

49.

I removed a handbag embroidered with beads from the drawer in the front desk and took it and lay it on top of the young woman's corpse.

I stayed there for a while, leaning against the wall, waiting to see if the young woman would wake up again.

The young woman never woke up.

50.

I'm at "The Poetry School" now.

The room is dark.

Just a moment ago I heard the pipes glumpglomping on the other side of the wall. Vampires are funny, aren't they?

51.

Laying my pen down on the desk, I stood up from my chair, and yawned.

There's really nothing left for me to write.

I've finally managed to catch up with the present.

52.

Right now, I feel as nice as I possibly could.

I was a gangster. I was never a poet. I've been a gangster ever since I was born.
And I'm about to prove it.
I'll put a bullet into my heart, and then I'll wake up feeling so nice, so, so nice.

I know it now.
Now that things are so nice.
That I'm a gangster, which is nice, nice, nicer than anything.

Epilogue

The body of "The Crippled Gangster" was on display in front of City Hall.

The boys who came to see it were disappointed.

Because the corpse was rotting.

"I thought gangsters' bodies weren't supposed to rot," said one.

"Yeah, this one must be some kind of fake," said another.

"Man oh man, a rotting gangster isn't nice at all."

"Ugh, a rotting, fake gangster. Screw this."

And the boys wandered slowly off toward a place with something nicer.

Works Cited

Page 34   Aristotle; *The Complete Works of Aristotle*; translated and edited by Jonathan Barnes; Princeton University Press; 1984.

Page 40-41 Terayama, Shuji; *Kentakkii Daabii Kansenki*; Kadokawa Shoten.

Page 63   Joyce, James; *Finnegan's Wake.*

Page 63   Chikamatsu, Monzaemon; *Sonezaki Shinju*; translated by Donald Keene; in *Anthology of Japanese Literature*; edited by Donald Keene; Grove Press; 1955.

Page 65   Koguma, Hideo; "Amiwatari no Genjitsu"; in *Tobu Sori*; Shichosha.

Page 76   Tanikawa, Shuntaro; "Arisu"; in *Sono Hoka ni*; Shueisha; 1979.

Page 112   Sandburg, Carl; "Tentative (First Model) Definitions of Poetry"; in *The Complete Poems of Carl Sandburg*; Harcourt Brace Jovanovich; 1970.

Page 160   Suzuki, Shiroyasu; "Kanzen Muketsu Shinbun Sosetsu Kidan"; in *Kanzen Muketsu Shinbun Tofuya Ban*; Shichosha.

Page 194-95 Oshima, Yumiko; "Mada Yoi no Kuchi"; in *Oshima Yumiko Kessaku-sen*; Kabushiki-gaisha Sanrio; 1978.

Page 199   Huyghe, Rene; *Ideas and Images in World Art*: *Dialogue with the Visible*; translated by Norbert Guterman; Harry N. Abrams, Inc.; 1959.

Page 214   Rilke, Rainer Maria; *Rainer Maria Rilke: Poems 1906 to 1926*; translated by J.B. Leishman; New Directions; 1957.

ABOUT THE AUTHOR

Genichiro Takahashi, b. 1951, never graduated from Yokohama National University. As a student radical, he was arrested and spent half a year in prison, a harrowing experience that rendered him incapable of reading or writing for several years. *Sayonara, Gangsters* took the literary establishment by storm and remains one of the summits of postmodern writing in Japanese or any other language. Other novels by Takahashi include *John Lennon vs. The Martians, A*D*U*L*T*, and *The Rise and Fall of Japanese Literature*. Also a literary critic, he is the author of *The Maybe-It's-Not-Literature Syndrome* and other popular collections. Winner of the Mishima and other coveted literary awards, Takahashi has been the best-kept secret of readers of Japanese. *Sayonara, Gangsters* is his first full-length work to be published in English.

*

Michael Emmerich has translated works by Yasunari Kawabata and Banana Yoshimoto. He lives in New York City.

Whether you like Japanese stuff

READ

For those unfamiliar with contemporary Japanese fiction, here is a quick overview of some of the most absorbing writing in Japan today – all available in translation from Vertical!

Gangster noir
***Ashes* by Kenzo Kitakata**
"*Ashes* depicts yakuza life with a unique understanding and edge-of-your-seat reality."
–*Midwest Book Review*

New age mystery
***Outlet* by Randy Taguchi**
"Her sexual encounters may have a healing power...and the novel's dark twists and turns should keep readers hooked until the surprising climax."
–*Publishers Weekly*

or just like good books,

DIFFERENT
READ

**V
E
R
T
I
C
A
L.**

Comedy of manners
Twinkle Twinkle by Kaori Ekuni
"This book is simple. This book is a pearl. This book is like water, clear and loose and natural and fluid." *–BUST magazine*

Ghost story
Strangers by Taichi Yamada
"An eerie ghost story written with hypnotic clarity. He is among the best Japanese writers I have read." –Bret Easton Ellis, author of *American Psycho*

Fantasy epic
The Guin Saga by Kaoru Kurimoto
"Readers should be cautioned that once you start this journey, it will be nearly impossible to leave it unfinished." *–SFRevu*